Carl Weber's Kingpins:

Dallas

Carl Weber's Kingpins:

Dallas

Treasure Hernandez

www.urbanbooks.net

Urban Books, LLC
300 Farmingdale Road, NY-Route 109
Farmingdale, NY 11735

Carl Weber's Kingpins: Dallas

ISBN 13: 978-1-945855-60-3
ISBN 10: 1-945855-60-6

First Mass Market Printing November 2018
First Trade Paperback Printing April 2018
Printed in the United States of America

10 9 8 7 6 5 4 3 2 1

This is a work of fiction. Any references or similarities to actual events, real people, living or dead, or to real locales are intended to give the novel a sense of reality. Any similarity in other names, characters, places, and incidents is entirely coincidental.

Distributed by Kensington Publishing Corp.
Submit orders to:
Customer Service
400 Hahn Road
Westminster, MD 21157-4627
Phone: 1-800-733-3000
Fax: 1-800-659-2436

Carl Weber's Kingpins:

Dallas

Treasure Hernandez

Prologue

"Oh my God! Lingerie? Seriously, Ti Ti?"

Tiara Rogers sat at a circular table watching her best friend open up the baby shower gift that she'd bought her.

"Well, shit! I figured since I'm going to be around buying the twins stuff anyways, I might as well take care of the mama!" She grinned at the sheer teddy and lace panties Elaya was holding in her hands. "I didn't know what sized titties you would have once you drop them babies, so there are like five bras at the bottom of the bag. Take your pick!"

The entire room burst into laughter, and Elaya cocked her head, rolling her eyes at her best friend.

"You're lucky I love you." She held the lingerie up one more time. "But hell, this will be motivation to snap back to my before-baby body! I'm ready for these chiren to come out and stop renting this one-bedroom belly!"

Tiara sat and beamed at the beautiful woman before her. Her heart ached in a good way just thinking about all of the things that Elaya had to endure just to get to her final stop of happiness. Her wedding ring glistened in the light, and the smile on her face was bigger than Tiara had ever seen it. When Elaya had opened her final gift and finally got tired of taking pictures, she came to where Tiara was sitting.

"You ain't right!" She pulled Tiara up by her hands. "You know I don't like people like that! Got me up there smiling and shit."

Elaya's full mocha-colored lips turned up as she made a face.

"Stop it," Tiara giggled. "I worked hard on your makeup, heffa, for you to be looking all ugly."

She took a step back and looked at Elaya. She looked like a goddess with a swooped band and a long braid that was tossed over her shoulder. Her breasts and butt looked amazing in the long, flowing white dress that laced her body. Her bright brown eyes shone, and it was almost impossible for her high cheekbones to show. The happiness just expelled from her eyes, and tears threatened to spill from Tiara's eyes.

"No!" Elaya pointed her finger into Tiara's face. "No tears! You promised. You spent hours on my makeup!"

But Tiara could not contain her joy. They had both lost everything, but at the same time, everything has finally fallen into place. The nightmare they had endured together was finally over. Elaya who had suffered the worst at the sick Doctor Pierce's hands had finally found happiness with a man who would never judge her. In Elaya, Tiara found something she had lost seemingly so long ago. Family. Despite Lay's warning, Tiara poked her full lip out and furrowed her brow as she looked at her friend with watery eyes.

"I'm sorry," Tiara said. "I just love you so much. He almost killed us."

"I love you too, Ti Ti. If it weren't for you, I would not have survived," Elaya said, trying to blink back her tears. "Aww, shit; fuck it."

They embraced each other and cried softly into each other's necks. Tiara felt one of the babies kick on her stomach and smiled through her tears.

I love you, little babies, *she thought.*

"Somebody get a clean-up team on aisle five. We have two beautiful women crying a river," Elaya's husband Clarence came up from the side of them. "Tiara, what I tell you about coming around starting trouble?"

The women laughed and pulled away from each other. Elaya swatted playfully at him and went over to give him a kiss.

"Shut yo' ass up, Clarence," Tiara grinned at him. "If it weren't for me, the two of you wouldn't be married or have these wonderful babies on the way! I'm the one who told her to say yes to that first date. Tell him, Lay!"

Elaya gave Clarence a look and raised her eyebrow. "She does have a point."

"Oh really?"

"Yeah, I thought you were weird looking at first."

The three of them cracked up laughing, and Tiara took a step backward to give them their personal space.

"Aye, T!" *Clarence said before she could get too far.* "There's a dude I went to college with over there by the punch. He said he knows you from back in the day. Go holla at him with your lonely ass. You know you need a man."

"Clarence!" *Elaya punched him in the arm.*

"What?" *He looked seriously confused about why she just hit him.* "You the one who said it!"

Tiara squinted her eyes at both of them, and Elaya guiltily shrugged her shoulders.

"It won't hurt to see what's up with him . . . right?"

"Uh-huh," Tiara said and made her way toward the refreshments table.

She wondered who on earth could possibly know her. She wasn't quite the friendliest person in high school, and the only person she was cool with back then was dead. Standing beside the table sipping virgin strawberry daiquiris was a well-built, chocolate man. He was muscular, tall, and looked like he would be quite edible once he took off his clothes. He was dressed simply in a pair of Levi khakis, a fitted black floral button up, and a fedora sat comfortably on his fresh haircut.

Damn this nigga is fine, she thought and subconsciously tucked her freshly flat-ironed hair behind her ear.

She too was wearing a white flowing dress to match her best friend that her body looked great in. When his eyes lay on her, he began to smile from ear to ear.

"Hey," she said when she reached him.

"I know who you are," he said, grabbing a cup with juice in it and handing it to her. "I don't expect you to remember me, though; you were way too popping back in high school."

"High school?" she asked and tried to study his face. All she saw was "fine," but nothing that she remembered.

"Yeah, that was a long time ago, though, so no worries."

"No, no," she shook her head and flashed a charming smile. "Tell me your name. I don't want to be rude."

"Stevelle Lawson, I used to kick it with Kent and them back in the day."

"Stevelle," she said, cocking her head trying to remember. "Stevelle . . . Stevelle . . . Stevelle! Oh my God!"

She grinned because suddenly she did remember who he was. Back then, he was just a skinny, tall kid, though. Like he said, he wasn't somebody that she would give a second glance at then. But now? She would love to give him a go.

"You were just a skinny kid back then; I see you got your weight up!"

"Stop it!" he said, grinning at her joke. "I see you're still as beautiful as you were back then."

The way he was looking at her made her face get hot, and she started to play with the cup he'd just handed her. She hadn't let a man get close enough to her to make her feel the way he was in ages.

"Thank you," was all she could think of to say.

"You're welcome. Shit, I'm surprised you really remember a nigga, being the kingpin's daughter and all."

At the mention of her father's name, the smile instantly wiped from her face. She looked at the ground and tried to mentally shut the doors that he'd just opened.

"My bad," he said, seeing her demeanor change. "I ain't mean to—"

"No, it's OK," she put her hand up. "Don't worry about it."

"I'm sorry about what happened to him. When I heard it, it fucked me up. He always showed love to the streets. They were never the same without him."

"Yeah," Tia stared sadly at her cup for a second. "He was a real good man. He didn't deserve that. Anyway, what have you been up to?"

Stevelle gave her a sly smile. "I have a few business ventures."

"Oh, I know what that means!" The smile was back on Tiara's face as she laughed at his words. "You a street pharmacist, huh?"

"Nah," Stevelle said, shaking his head, but, of course, Tiara didn't believe him.

The two spent the rest of the baby shower sipping virgin strawberry daiquiris and dancing until it was time to clean up and go home. They exchanged numbers when she walked him to his car. He was about to get into his all-white

BMW 328i when he suddenly turned back to her.

"I don't see a point in driving off, and then calling you to ask you something that I can do right now."

"What are you talking about?"

"I'm tryna see you later. You got me smiling and stuff. I haven't had this much fun with a girl in a long time. Can I pick you up in a few hours?"

Tiara's answer was the smile that spread on her face. She nodded her head. "Here," she said, pulling her phone back out and sent him a text. "I'll send you my address. I would ask you where you're taking me, but I'd rather just let you surprise me."

"A'ight, shorty." He checked his phone to make sure he got her message. "I'll see you later then."

He got in his car and drove off, leaving Tiara to walk back in the building smiling to herself. After what Doctor Pierce had done to her, she never thought she'd be able to look at another man the same. Yet, the way Stevelle looked at her, she didn't get one bad vibe from him. It had been awhile, and she knew it was time for her to finally get back out there on the dating scene.

She returned inside of the building, and the first thing she saw was Elaya still smiling from ear to ear. She watched her friend fall effortlessly into her husband's arms and couldn't help the pang that came suddenly in her stomach. The happiness that Stevelle had given her was short lived because right then, she couldn't help but feel as if she was missing something. Like there was an emptiness eating away at her heart. As she stared at her friend dancing, she could tell that she was at peace; however, she herself was feeling a void. She hadn't made peace with her past, but she was OK with moving forward with her future. Along with being part owner of A&E, an organization to help battered women and victims of sexual assault, Tiara had gotten a full-time job doing customer service for a phone company. She also had put herself up in her own one-bedroom apartment. She refused to beg her mother's people for help. She wasn't ready to face them yet, and she wouldn't be able to face them for years to come. It was her mother who had signed her off to Doctor Pierce in the first place because she couldn't bear looking at Tiara's face anymore. She wouldn't be trusting her for a while. She broke her eyes away from the dancing couple and finished packing up everything they'd brought with them and put it all into Clarence's SUV. Before she left, she gave Elaya one last big hug, promising to meet up again sometime that week for dinner or shopping.

"Are you sure you don't want a ride?" Elaya asked with concern dripping in her tone.

"No," Tiara told her, kissing her cheek. "I'll just catch a taxi. It's OK. You need to go straight home. You've done enough for today. I'll call you as soon as I make it in, OK?"

"OK," Elaya said and got into Clarence's vehicle. She blew Tiara a kiss before Clarence pulled off. Tiara didn't have long to wait before the cab pulled up to take her home. She got in and verified her home address so that the driver could take her to where her bed was located. Tiara held her Michael Kors over-the-shoulder bag tightly and listened to the cabdriver talk to himself as he drove. After a few minutes of listening, she soon figured out he wasn't talking to himself. She saw his headphones in his ears.

This motherfucker is on the phone and driving, *Tiara thought.*

Instantly irritated, she cleared her throat, hoping that the older Caucasian man would hear her. He looked at her in the rearview mirror of the cab, and Tiara got the feeling that he was annoyed that she had interrupted his phone conversation.

"You do know that you aren't supposed to be on your phone and driving, right?" she asked. "And I hope you know that because you are putting my safety on the line, whatever that meter says at the end of this drive, I'm only paying you half of that."

The man looked dumbfounded for a moment, but before he could say anything back to her, Tiara held up her hand silencing him.

"Just drive, please," she said.

She knew the driver wished that he could kick her out of the car. But if he did, she would raise hell and fuck him up in the process. By looking in her eyes through the rearview mirror, she was sure that he could see that she had some craziness in her. He drove all the way to her residence, and when he got there, Tiara took a peek at the meter. It read that she owed just over twenty dollars. She pulled out a ten from her purse and threw it in the front seat.

"If I ever see you, I won't ever pick you up!" the angry taxi driver scoffed.

"Fuck you," Tiara said before she exited the vehicle. "If you want money, then you should act like it."

She slammed the door when she exited the vehicle, whipping her long hair in the process. And she flicked the driver off for good measure *before she made her way to the entrance of her apartment complex. There were a few people walking the street, but not many. Tiara used her key to get into the secured entryway, and before she went up the three flights of stairs to her apartment, she checked her mail.*

"Nothing but bills," she said to herself and sighed.

A&E helped fund her outlandish shopping addiction and kicking it with her friends while her job paid her bills. There was no extra money to live, like really live. She was almost twenty-two, and she knew it was time for her to make amends with the Rogers. She just didn't know when. She took the elevator all the way up to apartment number 313. Her apartment wasn't large and lavish the way she'd like it to be, but it was home, and she was proud of what she had.

She opened the door and threw the envelopes in her hand on the dining-room table. Then she locked the door behind her and began to strip off her clothes right by the doorway. Tiara wanted nothing more than to take a long, hot shower in her bathroom. All the lights in her apartment were off, and she made her way through it naked and based off of memory. Undisturbed, she flicked on her light. Suddenly she screamed, long and loud.

"Oh, what?" the man sitting on her bed said, smiling at her. "You look like you've seen a ghost, my dear Tiara."

"W-what are you doing here?" Tiara stammered, covering her chest and her crotch with her hands.

"No point in covering up," the intruder said, eyeing Tiara's perfect body. "I've seen it all before. Tasted it all before. Fucked it all before."

"Leave!" Tiara yelled, looking around frantically before she finally located a pink silk Victoria's Secret robe and put it on. "Get out!"

Tiara regretted not having any sort of weapon on her, not even a stun gun. Her heart was pounding, and she couldn't deny that she was terrified. The man sitting on her queen-size bed was the man who was responsible for her life being the way that it was. He had taken away her innocence at an early age and was responsible for hurting the people she held dearest to her heart.

"I'm afraid I can't do that," he said menacingly. His grin and the look in his eyes made her stomach drop. "You have a pretty high price on your head in the underworld."

He stood up from the bed, and Tiara took in his appearance. He was wearing a pair of 501 Levis and a Crooks and Castles sweatshirt, but tucked into his pants, Tiara took in the sight of the butt of a gun there. She backed herself into the farthest wall as he advanced on her. She prayed silently for herself and her best friends, hoping that they weren't next. Finally, he was directly in front of her, so close that she could smell the tacos he ate for lunch on his breath.

"Tiara Rogers," he said, using his pointer finger to gently brush against the cleavage showing through her robe, "responsible for the deaths of Blake Rogers and Doctor Pierce. How do you plea?"

"Fuck you," Tiara spat, realizing that she was going to die at the hands of the ingrate anyway. "You aren't even worthy to speak my name out loud."

"Worthy?" he said to her. "Do not forget that you spent a year being raped and molested by a man twice your age. You are nothing but a used-up whore."

His words cut Tiara deeply because she had spent the last three years trying to heal and get past that part of her life. It was a daily struggle for her having to deal with the nightmares that presented themselves nightly. Every night she saw an image of Doctor Pierce on top of her, pounding into her relentlessly. She recalled the feelings of pleasure and hatred that seemed *to intertwine together. She remembered the feeling of the drugs on the days she fought him off of her in the institute, and she often had flashbacks of the day three of his workers ran a train on her. What she was having a hard time understanding was how the man before her had even the slightest clue of what was going on in the clinic.*

"Why are you here? What do you want from me?" Tiara did her best to sound confident. She refused to let him see that she was actually terrified inside. Don't show him that you're scared. You've been through worse shit than this. *Tiara gave herself a little pep talk. She tried to mentally prepare herself for whatever was about to happen.*

With one swift motion, he pulled out his gun and put it to her head. "This might just be one of the easiest hits that I've ever had to carry out since your father's," he said. "I just want you to know that back then, none of what I told you was a lie. You were always special to me. Now, it's just business."

At that moment his finger tightened around the trigger of his weapon and right before the shot rang out that would end her life, Tiara closed her eyes and took a deep breath when she felt the cold steel metal push against her temple. She had no regrets, so as she stood there vulnerable and unarmed, she prepared herself to die. She knew death would be coming for her one day. She wasn't expecting it to come to her so soon, but either way, here it was. Her mind rewound all the way back to the beginning of it all . . .

Chapter 1

"Death is only the beginning," an unforgiving voice spoke softly.

The lights inside of an empty two-car garage were dimmed, and the smell of old oil invaded the nostrils of a man sitting bound to a wooden chair. Five men stood around him like a pack of hungry wolves, their eyes begging him to do something stupid, although the only thing that he could do was quiver and look hopeless. He had already tried to plead his innocence, but his words fell on deaf and uncaring ears. There were footsteps on his right, and in seconds, there was a familiar figure standing in front of him. He looked into the eyes of the muscular man before him and felt that he was staring at the Grim Reaper himself.

Blake Rogers stood directly in front of the terrified man with murder in his eyes. The only thing separating the two of them was a table. On top of that table was a silver tray that held two items: a syringe and a meat cleaver.

"I trusted you, Vincent," Blake spoke again. "You are my cousin, but I loved you like a brother. Why would you steal from me? From my office? You must have thought by taking the security footage from my home, your tracks would be covered. Are you stupid, nigga?"

Blake had never felt more betrayed in his life. Not only was he missing a grand total of $150,000 from his home safe, but the offender was none other than his own flesh and blood. One of his most trusted workers informed him that he saw Vincent take the money with his own eyes. He claimed that the only reason he did not stop him was because Vincent said that he was following Blake's orders shortly after Vincent left town for a few days, and Blake hadn't heard from him.

This nigg knows how I get down. He musta been smoking something to pull this shit.

As Blake spoke, he grabbed the syringe and thumped the needle with the middle finger in his right hand. Vincent, whose mouth was duct taped shut, tried to scream, but the sound was muffled. Seeing the fury in Blake's eyes, Vincent fought hard against his restraints and made silent pleas with his eyes. Blake laughed out loud at the sound Vincent was making.

"Whose idea was the duct tape?" he asked with a thick Southern accent. He looked around at the circle of men, and his eyes fell on the one, Diablo, who had come forth with the news of the betrayal. He nodded his approval. "Good job. Can't have all of Texas hearing the cries of this scumbag, can we?" Blake said, thumping the needle with his finger. "You have been working with me for years, Vincent. Years! You've seen firsthand what happens to those who cross me. You have assisted with it! You are the only person who knew the combination to the safe, and Diablo here says he saw you taking the money out from my safe with a suitcase."

Vincent's eyes opened even wider, and he whipped his head so that he could face Diablo, who, in turn, smirked at him. His brow furrowed, and he shook his head "No," trying to plead his case, but the duct tape over his mouth prevented his speech. He fought so hard against the ropes around his arms and ankles that the chair shook back and forth. Finally, Vincent gave up, knowing that fighting was no use. There was no point in trying to plead for his innocence because Blake was too far past the point of reason. Instead, he said a silent prayer that God would have mercy on Diablo's soul.

"This, my dear cousin . . ." Blake nodded his head toward the needle that he was holding. He spoke so icily that he once again demanded Vincent's attention, "is rat poison. I want you to witness and *feel* every horrific thing that I'm about to do to your body."

Without a warning, Blake reached over the table, jabbed the needle into Vincent's neck, and released the poison into his body. It didn't take too long for Vincent to start feeling the effects of it coursing through his veins. He began to lose the ability to move his body parts. Within minutes, the only thing Vincent was able to move were his eyes, and Blake set the syringe down to grab the meat cleaver. His anger got the best of him, and he kicked the table between them out of the way. With a loud clank, the silver tray hit the ground, and Blake got in Vincent's face.

"Did you think I wouldn't find out that you've been stealing hundreds of thousands of dollars from me for years? After Diablo brought this shit to my attention, I had my accountant check all of my numbers—and lo and behold, it turns out that almost half a million dollars has gone missing from right under my nose! I never questioned giving you any of the codes to any of my safes or access to any of my bank accounts because I trusted you. We were raised like brothers!"

Blake brought the cleaver down so hard on Vincent's knee that everyone in the garage heard the bone crack upon impact. Vincent had no choice but to stomach the pain. He clenched his eyes shut, and a pained groan erupted from his throat. When he opened his eyes, tears spilled from them, and they fell on his limp leg. Blake hit the broken bone again with just as much force, and Vincent screamed like a tortured animal through his sealed lips trying to catch his breath. Blake backed away and went to the shelve in the garage that had all of the tools. Vincent used that time to gather his wits and glare once more at Diablo. He couldn't believe this was happening. His chest was heaving, and he wanted to do nothing but to pass out, although he was sure Blake wouldn't allow that. What had just started was only the beginning of Blake's torture. He knew how his cousin operated. He was able to take another breath just before he heard the sound of chains dragging on the ground. He looked up in time to see a metal chain being hurdled toward his face right before he felt the pain.

Unknown to all of the men in the garage, their every move was being watched by a set of tiny eyes. Nine-year-old Tiara Rogers stared at the horrendous act her father was performing from behind a tall trash bin. Her lips quivered and shook as she bit down to keep her whimper from coming up. She had been asleep for a while until she had heard suspicious sounds coming from the garage of their raised two-story, ranch-style, five-bedroom home. It hadn't been the first time she had heard noises of pain and suffering coming from the garage, but that night, something made her get up from the bed. Her mother would have a fit if she knew that her baby girl was sneaking around spying, which was why Tiara knew she would have to be as silent and quick as possible. She swore that her mother had eyes in the back of her head and bionic hearing.

Tiara wrapped the silk robe that her grandmother had given her for her last birthday around her petite body and hurried out of her room. When she passed her parents' bedroom, she peeked in to see what her mother was doing, but quickly saw that she was fast asleep with plugs positioned snugly in her ears. Tiara knew what that meant. Whenever her father thought that it might get a little noisy at night, he told her mother to wear them to sleep. Knowing that the coast was clear, Tiara walked fast through the house until she got to the spacious kitchen of their home. There, the door leading to the garage was open just a slit, enough for her to slide through the opening without having to touch it and be seen. She ducked down and got on all fours so that she could crawl behind the family's tall black garbage bin. The horrible smell suddenly reminded her that she was supposed to take it to the curb. The trash men would be there in the wee hours of the morning. Tiara made a mental note to do that before her mother found out that she had forgotten to do one of her chores.

Tiara heard her father speaking to her cousin Vincent, and her heart beat fast at the accusations she was hearing being directed at him. She peeked around the bin to look at the gruesome scene beginning to unravel itself, and she looked helplessly at Vincent, who she loved dearly, almost as much as she loved her own father.

"Stop, Daddy," Tiara whispered to herself trying to will her father to stop the attack, but he did the exact opposite.

Tiara put her shaking fingers to her mouth trying to decide what to do. She knew that if she made her presence known, she would be in big trouble with her father. But he needed to know that the man who had betrayed his trust was indeed in the garage, but it was not the man who he had strapped to the chair. Tiara knew for a fact that it was not Vincent who had stolen Blake's money from the safe in his office. She remembered the day perfectly.

She was dropped off early from soccer practice by one of the neighboring parents and nobody important was home yet, only the maids. They were doing what they always did when they thought nobody was home . . . standing in the backyard smoking marijuana. Tiara was thrilled to have the house to herself. That meant she could sneak some ice cream and watch an R-rated movie before her parents arrived home. As she was sitting in front of the sixty-inch floor television in the family room of the home her father had built from the ground up, she heard footsteps coming from upstairs. Tiara had never been the type to run from danger. She was the type of kid to go check out what was going on. Standing up, she set her almost-empty bowl of cookies-n-cream to the side and wiped her hands off on her soccer shorts. Walking to the stairs, she slowly crept and made her way up. As she got closer to the top steps, she stretched her neck to see who was cutting into her time. When she finally made it to the second level, the noises got louder and more distinct. They were coming from her father's office, and Tiara knew that her father wasn't there. She also knew that nobody was allowed in her father's office—only her cousin, who she viewed more as an uncle.

"Cousin Vincent?" Tiara's high-pitched voice called, assuming that it was him.

She pushed the door open to see who exactly it was in the office, but as she pushed, someone pulled. Tiara was shocked at the face she saw on the other side of the door. It wasn't her father or Vincent. It was another one of Blake's trusted hands, Diablo. Tiara looked at him with a confused look frozen on her young and innocent face. He looked just as shocked to see her as she was to see him, but he quickly recovered.

"*Lo siento mucho!* I'm so sorry, Princess," he flashed her a charming smile. "I did not know anyone would be home."

"What are you doing in my dad's office?" Tiara asked, her eyes finally landing on the black bag hanging from Diablo's shoulder. It was slightly open, and Tiara was able to peer inside and see what was there. Her eyes widened.

Diablo noticed her alarm and thought fast. "Your father and I were out in the . . . um," he cleared his throat. "In the field, and he needed me to run here and grab a few things for him. His hands are tied up at the moment. We all know how busy your father gets." He gave a small laugh.

"He's waiting for me, and I don't want to keep him waiting." He stepped out of the office and shut the locked door back before Tiara could get a good look at what was behind him. She did, however, notice that he had a small disk in his hand. "Would you like me to tell him you are home alone?"

Tiara quickly forgot her suspicions and shook her head fast. "No, that's OK," she said. "My mom should be home soon."

With that, Diablo planted a kiss to her forehead and walked past her to the steps and headed for the front door.

"See you at dinner on Sunday, Princess!" He called to her over his shoulder right before the door slammed shut.

After that, Tiara put the incident to the back of her mind, but that night as she was perched behind the stinky trash, the images of Diablo leaving Blake's office with a bag full of cash just didn't add up. Tiara felt tears falling down her already beautiful face when she saw how helpless her cousin was. She understood why Diablo stood there looking like he had won the lottery, and she also knew why he had given her father the idea to tape his mouth shut. It wasn't so that Texas couldn't hear his cries. It was so that he couldn't tell who the culprit really was.

Tiara watched her father hit Vincent a few more times, but soon, the blood got to be too much for her to bear.

"Daddy!" she yelled and jumped up from behind the trash can in the corner. "Stop it!"

Blake was so shocked to hear Tiara's voice, the familiar voice of his princess, that he stopped his attack on Vincent's face in mid-whip. Turning his head, he saw his beautiful baby girl standing behind him with tear streaks on her face. The face that mirrored his exactly. The men surrounding Vincent didn't miss a beat. They stood in front of Vincent in hopes to shield her eyes from seeing the shape that he was in, but it was too late. She had already seen enough, and the horrified look in her eyes told Blake just that.

"Tiara," Blake said, shaking his head, "what are you doing out of bed, sweetheart?"

"I heard noises," Tiara said. "I heard screams . . . I heard . . . Oh, Daddy, what are you doing to Vincent?"

Blake turned his head back to Vincent, whose head was nodding as he tried to stay conscious. Blake could lie to his child all he wanted, but unlike most kids her age, Tiara wasn't stupid.

"This is what happens to anyone who betrays your father," he told her. "Cousin Vincent has been a very bad man, baby. And now, he has to pay the cost. But you know you are not supposed to be out of bed once it's bedtime. Take her back to her room." He motioned for one of the men to escort Tiara back to her bedroom.

Tiara backed away from the advancing man, and her bare foot stepped into something cold and wet. She looked down and saw that she was standing in a small puddle of blood on the concrete floor. She knew that if she didn't speak her peace right now, her innocent cousin would be dead.

"Daddy, it wasn't Cousin Vincent!" Tiara looked up and glared at Diablo, who looked like he had just seen a ghost.

"Somebody get her to bed," Diablo said, hoping that someone would listen to him and not her. "Now!"

Tiara snatched away from her father's henchmen.

"It wasn't Vincent, Daddy!" she had started to sob uncontrollably. "The other day, Mrs. Sanchez dropped me off early from soccer practice, and I saw Diablo coming from your office with a bag of money, Daddy! You have to believe me!"

Tiara ran past the men to a bloody Vincent and stood with her arms spread wide. "You can't hurt him anymore!" she screamed. "I won't let you!"

Blake stood there in pure shock and pulled his pistol from his waist. The murderous stare that had once been on Vincent was now targeted to Diablo.

"Is this true?"

Diablo's voice betrayed him when he tried to answer, and nothing came out. His plan had just unfolded right before his eyes, and he knew that the cat was out of the bag. He didn't know what to say.

"Boss, I—" he started, but Blake silenced that with one shot to his knee.

Diablo dropped instantly to the ground crying in agony. The pain from the bullet and the impact from the fall knocked the wind out of him, and he rolled over onto his back trying to nurse his knee.

"So you would have me kill my own blood in rage?" Blake's voice was lethal. "Behind your treacherous acts of betrayal?"

Blake shot Diablo's other knee, and his screams caused Tiara to jump. Seeing this, Blake went to Diablo and kicked him in his face.

"Shut the fuck up," he said. "You are scaring my daughter. Get this son of a bitch out of here. Hog-tie him to the heaviest weight you can find and throw him into a river."

"And his family, boss?"

"Fuck his family," Blake said. "Make sure they are removed from my property and my neighborhood by morning."

Blake looked back at Tiara, who was touching Vincent's caramel cheek gently. She removed the tape from his mouth as softly as her delicate nine-year-old fingers could, but it still stung.

"Sorry, Cousin," she whispered when he jumped slightly.

"Thank you," Vincent's voice was barely audible and was drenched with pain. "Thank you so much."

"Daddy," Tiara told her father, "he needs to go to the hospital. You messed him up pretty good."

Blake walked over to his favorite cousin with regret and sorrow weighing heavily on his chest. He took his cousin's bloody hand, but before he could speak, he felt Vincent squeeze.

"N—no apology needed," Vincent smiled awkwardly up at Blake through bloody, busted lips. "A boss first. J—just get me to the hospital."

"I will make this up to you," Blake promised. "You will have every dime of what you were accused of stealing waiting for you in your bank account when you recover from this."

He wasn't sure if Vincent had heard him or not because he chose that moment to pass out.

But it didn't matter because Blake would make good on his word. Blake's men cut Vincent free and gently carried him out of the garage. Blake would pay whatever the cost to get Vincent back in shape. He should have known that he would never cross him like that. Diablo was closest to Vincent when it came to work. He had access to almost as much knowledge on Blake's operation as Vincent; therefore, he must have hacked into some information to steal the money, and it must have been going on for years. Blake made a mental note to open up all new accounts and change the combinations to all of his locks.

"You almost killed him, Daddy!" Tiara's voice interrupted Blake's thoughts. "You almost killed Vincent!"

Blake gripped Tiara's shoulders and knelt down so that they were at eye level. He sighed. "My child, I never wanted you to see any of this, but since you have, I want to be all the way honest with you. This may or may not be the last time you see such an act. One day you will understand, just as Vincent understands what has happened here. Sometimes you have to cut off your fingers to save your hand for the greater good of business. But I will forever be thankful that you intervened tonight. I love you, Princess."

His words that night would stay with her forever. She blinked back the tears and allowed her father to kiss her forehead. Blake stood up, grabbing his only child's small hand, and the two exited the now-empty garage and headed back into the warmth of their home. Tiara looked back at the chair that Vincent was once strapped to and all the blood surrounding it, knowing that it was an image that she might need to get used to seeing.

Chapter 2

As Tiara grew up, she became a very difficult child. She stopped listening to her mother and father's discipline the day she turned thirteen, but she didn't let her parents know that. To their faces, she made it seem like their word was law, but as soon as they were out of eye and earshot, she became the real her. She was the only child, and most days, it was just her and the housekeepers at home. When her father was out handling business in the streets, her mother Cat, short for Catera, was trying to find her purpose. Being the wife of a kingpin was not one of the things that she had on her bucket list; it's just the way things ended up playing out. She wasn't even ready to have a child, and that was why Tiara was her first, and only, one. She made small attempts to have some sort of relationship with Tiara, but truth be told, she never really cared about it. She was one of those "for show" parents. On her social media profiles, it seemed like she was Mom of the Year. But if only those people could see beyond the flawless makeup and designer bags, they would see that Cat hadn't taken Tiara on a trip alone since she was twelve, but she had gone on at least three by herself every year since.

Sometimes she would ask Tiara if she wanted to go to the movies or to dinner, and Tiara would have to check her. Going to the movies or going out to dinner when she didn't have plans didn't cut it. Her mother thought that putting forth minimal effort was enough, but it wasn't anywhere near enough. Tiara was jealous of the girls in her middle school class who came to school talking about how much fun they had with their parents and the trips they took. Tiara, of course, took trips with her parents, but they were always interrupted with her father's business calls or the fact that her mother simply just wanted to get away from both of them. The only time she really got to see her parents were on the Sundays her mother decided to have Sunday dinner. It was all beginning to take a toll on Tiara, and the only one who seemed to notice was her personal housekeeper, Stephanie. Stephanie had been overseeing Tiara since she was a baby, and when she noticed the change, she tried to bring it up to Cat.

The lady of the house was in the kitchen washing dishes, or that was what she called herself doing when Stephanie approached her. Stephanie and the other housekeepers would always have to go back over any cleaning job she did.

"Ma'am?" Stephanie spoke to Cat's back.

Hearing Stephanie's voice, Cat turned around, and when she saw the housekeeper's plump frame behind her, she gave her best fake smile.

"Hey, Stephanie," Cat said, drying her hands off on the dishrag that hung by the sink. "Does Tiara need anything?"

You're her mother. You should know what she needs, Stephanie thought and wanted to say, but she didn't.

"Why don't you know what your own child needs?"

"Because that's what I pay you for," Cat said, making a face at Stephanie.

"Well, she didn't come out of my vagina."

"Does *anything* come out of your vagina?"

Stephanie took in the image of the beautiful five-foot-four woman before her and wished she could just snatch the smug smile from off of her face. That was the issue with women who had money. They thought they were invincible. Stephanie knew she could take her, but the love she had for Tiara wouldn't allow her to lay a hand on Cat's head. She couldn't risk leaving the poor child alone with a mother like the one she had. The Christian Dior heels that Cat wore gave her a few more inches of height, and the sleek beige pantsuit clenched onto her fit body for dear life. Cat's face was blemish free, and although she was in her mid-thirties, she didn't look a day over twenty-five. Stephanie could not say that Cat was not beautiful. She felt as though that was all her head was wrapped around. The reason she never had another child was because she didn't want to ruin her body. She said it took her too long to bounce back after Tiara, and that she refused to put her body through that again.

"Um, kind of," Stephanie said. "Tiara does need something."

"Well," Cat put her hands in the air for emphasis, "what is it?"

"Tiara has been acting different ever since she started the eighth grade. Her teachers keep calling home and saying she's being a distraction in class. There have even been some fights. The only reason she hasn't been suspended or even expelled is because of who her father is and how much money he gives the school."

"OK, Stephanie. She's a kid. That's what kids her age do; they like to talk, and they fight."

"Yes, ma'am, I understand that, but the way she acts is not okay. The way she speaks, it's not right or appropriate for a girl her age to talk the way she does."

"Well, as you can see, Tiara isn't a normal girl her age."

"All I'm saying, *ma'am,* is that you and your husband might want to spend some quality time with her while you still can. I think you should form a better relationship with her."

Cat looked at Stephanie like she was a fly on the wall.

"*Who* do you think you are? Coming in here and telling me what *I* should do with my child? Are you her parent? And if it so important to you, why don't you just tell her this?"

Stephanie finally had enough. She looked at Cat with the same type of contempt in her eyes.

"No, but I might as well be! I have been taking care of her since she was a baby, and it is the truth when I say that all the things you take credit for, *I* taught her! These last few years of her life I have watched her grow, and each day she becomes sadder and sadder. If you paid half as much attention to her as you did to that foundation you put on your face every day, you would see this!"

Cat tried to speak, but Stephanie held her hand up to her to shut her up and continued speaking herself.

"Now, I can talk to that girl until I'm black and blue, but you see she didn't come from my womb, so I don't think it has the same effect. She doesn't feel loved, and she feels pushed to the side. This is the last year that you'll have her until she's gone from you forever. Once high school gets a hold on her, and she has *that* attitude? Not even the fact that her father is the most deadly man in this state will be able to put fear in that child's heart."

Stephanie left Cat standing there looking dumbfounded and went back upstairs to check on a sleeping Tiara. She could only hope that she'd gotten through to Cat and maybe she would pass the message on to Blake, but the next few weeks showed her that her words had once again fallen on deaf ears. The saying you could lead a horse to water but you could not force it to drink was absolutely true. The warning Stephanie had given was one that should have been heeded. She knew how it went; she was the eldest of five children. She had seen it all. She also knew that once a good girl turned bad, she was gone forever, and Tiara had already gotten a taste of that life.

The rest of Tiara's eighth-grade year Stephanie tried her best to keep her in check, but it was hard to do that when her father showered her with gifts just because. It was like she was getting rewarded for acting a fool. There was no positive or negative reinforcement because Tiara got everything she wanted, and even things that she didn't want. Stephanie knew the reason for the gifts were because Blake felt guilty from being so disconnected with his daughter, but everyone knew that Blake's first love was his business. He had left it up to everyone else to raise his child, but what he didn't understand was that although he had an iron grip on the streets and on his business, he had passed that same mentality on to his daughter. Not only did she look just like him, she had his mind as well. She was growing up with only herself to look to for guidance.

Stephanie knew that things had finally made a turn for the worse the day that she caught Tiara smoking marijuana in the bathroom of her bedroom. Stephanie was so caught off guard that she didn't know what to do when Tiara opened the door. Her eyes were low and bloodshot red.

"Tiara?" Stephanie called out to the thirteen-year-old.

In response, Tiara gave her a dopey smile and tried to shut the bathroom door behind her. But it was too late because Stephanie had already smelled the potent aroma and saw the smoke sneaking through the cracks.

"Oh my God," Stephanie exclaimed. "You're high as a freaking kite!"

"I'm OK, I'm OK," Tiara tried to assure her and went to lie down on her bed. "I feel so good right now. This was some really good weed. Hey, Stephanie? Have you ever wondered like . . . how caterpillars turn to butterflies? Or if they're even like . . . the same *person?* Well, bug. That's some trippy-ass shit!"

"Watch your mouth, young lady! Where did you get it from?"

Tiara made a noise that sounded like a scoff. She looked over at Stephanie with low eyes and burst into a fit of giggles.

"You know the other caregivers smoke on all of their breaks," she giggled and snuggled into her pillow. "I just snatched it from one of their bags. It's some good stuff too. Do you smoke weed, Steph?"

"*Por qué?*" Stephanie asked. "No, I don't smoke weed, and I don't feel the need to either. I like being able to think clearly, and I don't like to walk around with my eyes low looking like a damn fiend! Why do you feel the need to be high? How long have you been smoking?"

She went over to Tiara's bed as well and lay beside her in her work clothes. Tiara smelled strongly of the product and smoke, but that didn't stop Stephanie from pulling her close.

"My life sucks. Everybody thinks that it is just so cool to be the daughter of Blake Rogers just because he's rich. But it's not great at all! I just need something to balance out my lows, and weed does that for me," Tiara told her, and then started laughing like she had just told the world's funniest joke. "Nobody gives a fuck about me. You know it just like I know it. And I've been smoking for about five months now. I usually have eyedrops so you guys can never tell."

"Oh, honey," Stephanie just shook her head. "I feel like I'm losing you."

"You will never lose me, Steph," Tiara said while yawning. "But everyone else might as well have already said good-bye. I'm done aiming to please the two people who created me, especially when I'm invisible to them. They don't care about me . . . They only care about themselves. Well, it's time for me to start doing the same thing."

"Oh, honey," was all Stephanie could say.

She could chastise Tiara all that she wanted, but she knew that there would be no point. If she had been smoking for five months now,

Tiara had already made her choice. It was too late, and she knew whatever she said would just go over her pretty, curly head. It hurt Stephanie to know that the reason Tiara smoked was to numb the feeling of emptiness that she must have been feeling for so long.

After that incident, Stephanie tried her best to fill a little bit of that void over the next few years. She tried to get her out of the house and even tried to talk Tiara's father into letting her have some of the perks that normal teenagers had in high school. No kid wanted to feel like a prisoner in their own life. That was the quickest way to devalue your child. Tiara didn't know it, but in a way, her acting out was just a cry for attention. Stephanie tried hard to dote on Tiara, but what she soon found is that all she was doing was reminding Tiara that her parents weren't very active in her life.

After a while, however, Blake noticed how distant his daughter was from him her first few years of high school. He also noticed how slick her mouth was. He was constantly having to put her in her place. He was upset with Cat because she was supposed to be the stay-at-home parent and teach their daughter morals and values, but then again, he couldn't be too upset. The only family-oriented thing that she did was make dinner on some Sundays. He knew when he married her that she was too self-centered to be a mother. He knew Cat loved Tiara very much, but she just didn't know how to be a mother. It was easier letting the help do the job they were too busy to do.

Then the guilt set in once he realized that his only child was in high school, and he barely knew her. The housekeepers knew everything about her, but he still thought her favorite food was ice cream and cake. He knew it might be time to take a step back and handle his business behind the scenes versus up front and in person. He also knew that it might be too late, but he hoped that Tiara would give him a chance, which she did, and the two of them got very close. He learned that not only did she look like him, but she thought like him and acted like him as well.

Stephanie never told him about the weed, and she hoped that Tiara would be smart enough to hide it well from her father. He would kill them all if he knew his daughter was under the influence of anything. He had seen many things in the streets, and he truly believed that weed was a gateway drug. When that didn't do the job anymore, the person would be looking for the next best high. Cocaine.

It seemed like Tiara was well on her way back to herself since her relationship with her father was getting much better. He was excited for her to start her senior year of high school. He made a promise to her. He promised that as long as she remained boy free and stayed a virgin, then once she graduated high school, he would put $1 million in her bank account for her to do whatever she wanted with it. Tiara was happy with the proposition because she knew exactly what she wanted to do with that money. As soon as that money was put in her bank account, she planned on moving as far away from her parents as she possibly could.

Staying a virgin would be easy considering she didn't have too many guys approach her in school. Her father made sure nobody ever came close to her, and if they did, he had hired hands around her at all times who would tell him her every move. The only time she could flirt with guys was on social media, and even that was monitored. If she ever gave a boy her number, Blake would just call the cell phone company and block the number. She often felt like she was in jail and not at a place that she should call home. At first, boys would try to talk to her, but when word got around about who her family was, the boys from school completely backed off.

They were all too intimidated just because of who her father was. So when her father came to her with that proposition, she immediately agreed to it. Like a silly young, teenage girl, she made the promise that she shouldn't have.

Chapter 3

Beep! Beep!

"Noooo!" Seventeen-year-old Tiara moaned into her pillow. She cursed her alarm. "Shut the fuck up!"

She threw her covers back over her head, trying to block out the sun, only to have them pulled from her head.

"Oh no, you don't!" Tiara heard her personal housekeeper say. "You won't be late for another day of school. Your father chewed me out the last time that principal of yours called home."

Tiara smacked her lips.

"Please, Stephanie!" she begged. "Just ten more minutes? I went to sleep late last night."

"Nope," Stephanie said and made Tiara sit up. "Whose fault was that, huh? How many times have I told you not to go to sleep late on a school night? I bet you didn't even do your homework, did you? Isn't that science project due today?"

Stephanie continued to fuss at Tiara as she got the young girl's clothes prepared for the day. Tiara tuned the short, plump woman out and stretched her arms out as a large yawn escaped her mouth. Standing up, she forgot what was in her lap until it fell to the ground and rolled over and hit Stephanie's white-laced shoe. Tiara bit her lips together and raised her eyebrows, hoping that Stephanie wouldn't look down. She got no such luck. When Stephanie saw what had thumped against her foot, her hand flew to the apron covering her chest, and her nose twisted up.

"Tiara!"

"Well, now you know why I was up so late," Tiara stifled a laugh as she motioned to her vibrator lying by Stephanie's foot.

She shrugged, and Stephanie just shook her head. She spoke, but her tongue got lost somewhere in turning her mental thoughts into actual words.

"You're having sex, Tiara?" Stephanie asked, already knowing what Blake would do if he found out something like that.

"No," Tiara said with an attitude. She rolled her eyes, grabbing the underwear that Stephanie had placed on her queen-sized bed. "If I was, I wouldn't have to put that thing on my middle finger at night and rub my own puss—"

"My God, Tiara!" Stephanie threw her arms Tiara's way, making a face. "Why must you talk like that?"

"I'm just being honest. I haven't gone all the way with a boy yet, but I'm seventeen. I have womanly needs now. I'm sure you remember what it's like. At least I'm touching myself and not letting anyone else do it."

Stephanie couldn't help but to silently agree, but that still didn't mean she was satisfied. Tiara smirked and went to the bathroom to shower. When she was done, she came back out clean and wearing her undergarments. Her body was fully defined, and her brunette hair hung to the middle of her back. After she applied lotion to her cream-colored skin, she put her long hair into a high ponytail. Once her hair was in place, she put on her school uniform: blue pants, a white-collared blouse, and a gray sweater hung around her shoulders. The pants fit snugly around her waist, and her hips looked good.

"Ohhh! *Yesss!* My ass looks amazing in these pants!" She admired herself in the full-length mirror on her bedroom door.

Stephanie scooted Tiara out of the room and told her breakfast was on the table.

"You need to be out of the house by 7:00! I'm serious today, Tiara. Your car will be waiting out front." Tiara hurried down the stairs and made her way to the kitchen. She heard voices that belonged to her mother and her father already there, and she stopped to listen to their conversation.

"You really need to learn how to control your anger, Blake," Cat said to her husband. "Remember what happened with Vincent?"

Tiara remembered far too well, and she heard her father grunt.

"That is old news, my dear," Blake said to his wife. "Vincent has long since forgotten about that incident and has retained his position as my most trusted."

"Well, regardless of that, you need to get a handle on it. It's starting to get out of control."

"My anger is how I keep the control," Blake responded, and Tiara heard papers shake.

She smiled, knowing that her father was reading the newspaper and probably drinking a cup of coffee. She imagined her mother smiling at her father's smart mouth like she always did and saying . . .

"You get on my nerves," Cat said, just as Tiara thought it.

"I'm a man. That's what we do," Blake replied.

Tiara walked in on the two of them just as her father grabbed her mother in for a playful hug.

The two of them were still laughing when they finally noticed their child's presence. Blake sat wearing an all-black Versace suit that accented his muscular frame. His black hair that he rocked in a low cut had a few gray streaks, but that didn't take away from his youthful face. Many girls Tiara's age and women of all ages sent lustful eyes Blake's way, but he let everyone know that he only had eyes for one woman and that was his wife. He checked the gold Rolex on his wrist and gave a faux gasp.

"Who are you and what have you done with my daughter?" Blake said, letting go of Cat and picking up his newspaper again.

Tiara giggled and took her seat at the kitchen table. Although they had a dining room, her mother made sure to keep everyone out of it. Only on Sundays during Sunday dinner were people allowed to enter her sacred room. The kitchen area was spacious and every home-owner's dream. She had designed it a few years back, and everything had been custom built. It was equipped with state-of-the-art stain-less steel appliances. The cabinet doors were a deep mahogany with chrome-accent handles. The color scheme included many bright colors because Cat believed that subconsciously, bright colors made you happy. And since most people started their days in the kitchen, then they were bound to have a good day. Cat loved decorating and designing. It had always been a passion of hers. Over the years, she had put a lot of time and effort into redecorating the house to her liking. She had a vision for the whole house that she carried out effortlessly.

"I'm the same me, Daddy," Tiara said, staring down at the plate that was already filled in front of her. "You can thank Stephanie. She forced me to get up."

"Good," Blake said. "I've been thinking, it feels like I rarely see you anymore. How about I take you shopping this weekend before I head out to California?"

Tiara used her fork to scoot her bacon around the French toast on her plate. She knew her father would want a response, but she couldn't give him the one he wanted.

"Daddy, what's the point in going shopping when nobody will even see me in any of the beautiful things you buy me?" she said dully. "I still have tons of bags with clothes and jewelry that I haven't even worn yet."

"What do you mean nobody will see you in them? You have friends, don't you?"

"Yeah, but they ain't nobody. I never get to *really* go anywhere with the kids my age."

Blake sighed deeply knowing that she was right. But the last thing he needed was for anyone seeing Blake Rogers's daughter out and trying to get to him by harming her. He knew that growing up the only child of a drug kingpin couldn't have been easy, and Blake sympathized with her for that. But it was essential for him to keep an iron fist around her, even if it meant that she didn't have her own identity. School was the only getaway that she got, and for now, that was enough.

Tiara was convinced that no matter how much her parents loved her, they would never understand her. The way she thought was so much different than them, and it annoyed her that they acted as if she didn't know what was going on around her. She had seen firsthand what kind of man her father was at an early age. She knew what he was capable of. Every time Blake got free time, he thought that taking Tiara shopping would make up for all of the important events in her life that he had missed. But Tiara felt obliged to let him know that he couldn't buy her love. She also was annoyed by the fact that after all the time they'd spent together, she thought he'd known by now that material things meant nothing to her. That she wanted to see the world and do fun things like scuba dive and BASE jump.

To him, he thought they had a good relationship, but to Tiara, they couldn't have been on further ends of the totem pole.

Tiara looked at Cat who, instead of backing her up, placed her hand on Blake's shoulder and threw daggers with her eyes at her.

"Don't take that tone with your father, young lady! He works hard, and all he's saying is that he's wanting to spend some time with you! Most girls who have fathers like yours don't even get to see them at all because they're too busy!"

Blake held his hand up to calm Cat down, knowing that the approach she was taking wasn't the correct one.

"What is it that you want then, Tiara? What can you and I do together before I go to California?"

Tiara already knew what she wanted. "How about we go to the shooting range, and you can show me how to use a gun?"

Cat's right hand flew to her chest just as her left hand flew to her mouth. The woman was in disbelief of what her daughter had just asked of her father. Cat's mouth kept opening and closing while she tried to find the words to speak. Blake, on the other hand, had placed his chin on top of his clasped knuckles. He peered into his daughter's eyes and was almost surprised to see that they were empty. They reflected his perfectly. It alarmed him for the simple fact that he thought he'd done everything in his power to prevent exactly that from happening. Then again, she was born a Rogers. No matter how green he would like her to stay, it was her rite of passage to know the ways of a hustler.

"What else would you like for us to do?"

"We can go out to eat, and you can talk to me about how to make my own money."

Blake couldn't help but to laugh. The expression on her face let him know that she was dead serious. His brow furrowed, and he cocked his head. Never had his child intrigued him so much.

"Absolutely not!" Cat interjected when she found her voice again. "Hell, no. Shoot a gun? You must be out of your mind."

"Why not?"

"Because I said no, and you will listen to your mother!"

"My mother? Oh, you mean Stephanie?" Tiara glared at her mother. "She's upstairs. I can go ask her what she thinks if you want."

"Tiara!"

Blake's bark was lethal, and Tiara instantly stood down. Cat looked like somebody had just slapped her in the face, but Tiara felt no remorse for her words. Everybody in the room knew that they were nothing but the truth.

"Don't ever take that tone with your mother again, do you understand me?"

"Yes," Tiara grumbled, wanting nothing more than to give Cat a dirty look; instead, she just settled for rolling her eyes. She knew better than to go against her father's instructions.

"Good," Blake said and glanced back at his paper. "Now, you are dismissed. There is a car waiting to take you to school. And roll those eyes of yours again and I'll show you one of the many ways I can gouge them out. When you get home, I will be waiting, and your first gun lesson will start."

Tiara's face instantly lit up, and she jumped to her feet.

"Thanks, Daddy!" she said in his neck when she threw her arms around him.

"Now go! You're going to be late for school because you're trying to choke me."

He kissed her forehead before she pulled away and ran to the front door. When she got outside, sure enough, there was a black car waiting for her out front. It was still dark outside and even a little chilly, just like most mornings when she left for school. She looked around her neighborhood knowing that every house her eyes fell upon was her father's property. Before she was even born, Blake bought a large piece of land. On that land, he had ten houses built from the ground up. He rented them out to some of his family members and his most loyal workers. Around his land, there was a gate with a secured entrance, so in a way, he had created his own little community. One that he controlled and ruled effortlessly. There was nothing better than being surrounded by people that he both loved *and* trusted. The sun was beginning to shine now, and Tiara walked toward the black Audi Q5 waiting to drive her to school. Before she got to the car, her driver, Thomas, was already holding her door open for her to get in.

"Hello, Princess," Thomas said, smiling at Tiara. "You look delightful this morning."

Tiara muttered something rude under her breath, grabbing her own door and slamming it shut. She rolled the middle console up so that she wouldn't be forced into having conversation. The day had just started, and she was already completely over it. The only thing about the day that she was looking forward to was seeing her best friend, Brandy.

The second Thomas pulled up to the front of Tiara's school, she jumped out without saying good-bye and quickly blended in with the other kids hurrying to get into the building. Once she was certain that she was out of Thomas's eyesight, she pulled her hair out of the pony-tail it was in, letting it fall freely around her shoulders. Once she was through the tall, metal double doors, she made her way to her locker and applied her red MAC lipstick to her lips. Unbuttoning the top two buttons on her blouse, she arranged her shirt so that she could show off her cleavage. As she walked, she ignored the many girls trying to get her attention by complimenting her appearance. All she wanted to do was get to her regular morning spot.

Finally, she reached her locker, only to find a group of boys standing by it. Upon seeing her, they all gave her body lustful glances. One of them even had the nerve to lick his lips. She knew him only because he was in a few of her classes. His name was Kent something or other. He wasn't bad looking but definitely not her type. He was too light skinned and skinny for her. The best part about him were the neat cornrows in his long, great grade of hair.

"Nigga, don't be licking your lips at me," Tiara rolled her eyes at him.

"Damn, Tiara," Kent said. "My bad, but that ass gets fatter every day! You know you're the baddest in the whole school."

"I been knew that," she said, reaching into her Louis Vuitton backpack so that she could grab a piece of gum out of it and sexily put it in her mouth. "Is there a reason why you niggas are standing around my locker like a pack of wolves?"

She didn't really care about them standing near her locker, but she knew that her father had eyes and ears all throughout the school. Her wearing the lipstick she had on was already enough to get her in trouble. The last thing she needed was for one of his goons to snitch her out about talking to the boys at school.

"Mannnn," Kent said, dragging out the word. His eyes lit up like he was about to tell Tiara the story of the year. "So yesterday, right? My nigga Stevelle and that nigga Marco got into it about a bitch."

"Who?"

"Najay. That light-skinned girl in our algebra class."

"With the freckles?" Tiara asked, thinking about all the girls in her algebra class.

"Yup, her," Kent nodded. "Well, apparently, she been fucking my nigga Stevelle here," he patted a boy standing next to him on the arm. "And she been fucking Marco at the same time. Now that nigga wanna scrap, and Stevelle ain't no bitch. So we finna just get this shit popping right quick before class."

He shrugged his shoulders like it wasn't nothing. Tiara glanced at Stevelle and saw that he was just as skinny as Kent. He was darker in complexion, and the waves in his brush cut were deep enough to swim in. Tiara didn't know if she'd ever seen him around school, but she for sure had seen Marco. Marco was a caramel-skinned boy who was a senior just like them. He was buff and also was the star on the wrestling team. Tiara raised her eyebrows at Stevelle and just shook her head.

"You might as well just let that go," she said. "Ain't no ho worth getting your ass beat over."

"Who getting their ass beat?" Stevelle asked in a surprisingly deep voice.

"What's going on over here?" Tiara heard Brandy come up on the side of her.

"Girl, nothing," she said and gave her best friend a hug. "Just that these basic niggas are about to fight."

Brandy looked at the group of boys and shook her head. "I swear private school is worse than public school. You niggas are always acting a fool."

"You tryna stay and watch?"

"Hell, yeah, girl!" Brandy exclaimed. "I'm from the hood. Ain't nothing like a good fight."

Tiara laughed and dapped her friend up. Brandy was looking extra cute with her short hairstyle freshly tapered and an auburn track bang swooped to perfection in front of her face. Tiara was thick, but Brandy was what you would call voluptuous. She'd just turned eighteen, and her body followed suit. Her stomach was flat, and her hips were wide. She had natural 38C breasts and an apple bottom with a deep cuff. Her smooth cacao skin and pretty face made her stand out from all of the other girls in the school.

"Where this nigga Marco at though?" one of the boys standing in the group of six said.

"Yeah, man, where that boy at?"

"He ain't gon' show!"

Tiara hadn't noticed the crowd that had formed by her locker until then. Everyone was looking around, scanning the hallway for any sign of Marco. Tiara glanced at the clock and saw that they only had five minutes to get to class before the bell rang.

"C'mon, best friend," she said and grabbed Brandy's arm. "Let's get to class. These niggas faking."

As soon as the last word left her mouth, the crowd cleared, and Marco stepped forward. Behind him, like Stevelle, he had a group of his own friends to back him up. He looked square in Stevelle's face with a sneer of his own.

"I'm here, nigga," Marco said and yanked up his pants, squaring up with Stevelle. "What's up, homie? I heard you been tryna fuck with my bitch."

"Nah," Stevelle said, putting his fists up as well. "I ain't trying. I been *fucked* your bitch, and she sucked my dick. There's a difference. You can have her back, though. I'm done with that."

His words must have struck a nerve because Marco launched at Stevelle and tried to rock him with a strong right hook. Stevelle dodged it effortlessly and followed through with a right hook of his own. Marco had been leaning in, and his face was met with a surprisingly strong fist from Stevelle. His head snapped to the side, and he stumbled slightly. Stevelle used that to his advantage and plowed into Marco with a combination that not too many could come back from.

"Damn! How he getting rocked by that skinny dude?"

"Marco, get up!"

"Stick that nigga, Stevelle! You better not let that nigga get up!"

The crowd was going crazy at the fight going on in front of them. Nobody jumped in; they just let the guys handle their business. Marco tried to fight back as best as he could, but Stevelle had gotten the advantage. Marco had blood spewing from his nose and a gash over his eye before the sounds of the school's security broke up the crowd.

"Oh shit! C'mon, T!"

Brandy grabbed Tiara's hand before security could grab them up and ran in the direction of their first class. The final bell was ringing, and neither girl bothered to look behind them to see what was going on with the people they left behind. As Tiara ran, she spotted one of her dad's hired goons watching her at the end of the hallway. She groaned and put her head down and hit a sharp right with Brandy to run up a flight of steps. All she wanted to do was see a good fight, but she was sure that her father would know about that by the end of the day.

Up until two years ago, Blake had his daughter shadowed by security practically every minute of every day. He made one of his men follow her to every class, while another sat outside her classroom every single day. It was something the other kids talked badly about behind her back. Everyone thought she felt as if she was better than them, and that wasn't the case at all. If only they knew how jealous she was of their normal lives. After a lot of pleading and begging,

Tiara talked her father into cutting back on his extreme measures, and he had finally agreed to let her go to school without being followed around by his security. Blake wasn't too crazy about it, but he decided to compromise with his daughter. Instead of having someone walk her to class every day like a baby, they could just patrol the whole school while she was there. She told him she was almost a grown woman, and she needed to find her own sense of independence. It was hard to do that when everywhere she looked she was reminded of who her father was—and so was everyone else.

She refused to graduate high school without retaining any of the memories of a normal teenage girl. She vowed that her senior year would be different and, so far, it had been. She was enjoying her year thus far and had even figured out clever ways to sneak past her father's security goons so she could have some real fun with her friends and not have to worry about it all getting back to her father. Tiara wasn't a bad kid, but since school was the only time she really had to herself without having so many people peering over her every move, she took advantage of it. She often skipped class to hang out with her friends and do other things that she had no business doing.

Tiara walked into her first class, English, and shined her perfect teeth at Brandy before they both made their way to their side-by-side desks in the back of the classroom. Tiara started to make her way to the back of the classroom when she heard a loud whisper near her. She looked to her right and saw one of the girls, Ericka Towns.

"Here comes little miss prissy bitch," Ericka whispered to her friend. Ericka had hated Tiara since the first day Tiara started attending school there. Ericka had made the mistake of thinking that she and Tiara were in a competition. Unfortunately for her, Tiara had no competition. Ericka was just another hating-ass bitch like the next. Tiara decided not to acknowledge what she'd heard and instead, she walked passed Ericka, winked, and blew her a kiss before continuing on her way toward her desk.

"Stevelle beat the hell out of Marco!" Brandy whispered as soon as they sat down.

"Girl! With his skinny self." Tiara shook her head tucking her hair behind her ear. "Crazy thing is ole girl ain't even that bad."

"On my mom she's not," Brandy said. "I heard about their beef yesterday and couldn't believe it was over Najay. That bitch ass is flatter than a flapjack."

The girls shared a giggle.

"Hey, girl! Why didn't you call me back last night?" Brandy inquired.

Tiara thought back to the night before and how she'd gotten off the phone with Brandy so that she could watch porn and pleasure herself. After she had the most extreme orgasm ever, she passed out and hadn't woken up until Stephanie came in her room.

"I had some business to handle," Tiara said with a sly smile, and Brandy burst out laughing.

"Oh my God, girl," Brandy said, using her hand to wipe the tears from her eyes. "You are nasty. You need to just get some dick and stop playing with yourself. Literally!"

Tiara laughed too.

"It's not exactly that easy. You know who my daddy is." Tiara gave Brandy a knowing look. "He would kill me and whatever ingrate stuck his little penis in my coochie."

"Ti Ti!" Brandy laughed again. That time it made their teacher look their way.

"Are you ladies done talking so can I begin my lesson . . . Unless one of you wants to come up here and teach the class instead?"

"Sorry, Mrs. Ross," Brandy said. "We'll stop talking."

Mrs. Ross's eyes remained on Tiara, and she continued to glare at her. Tiara, already knowing where her teacher's dislike for her stemmed from, jerked her neck in disrespect and rolled her eyes.

"Is there a problem, Mrs. Ross?" Tiara asked. "We already said we were done talking. You can teach now."

Mrs. Ross curled her lip, and suddenly the whole class got quiet. She walked to the back of the class until she was directly in front of Tiara.

"Listen here, young lady," she said to the young girl. "I don't care who your father is outside of this classroom, but while you are here, you won't receive any special treatment. Do you understand me?"

Tiara looked at her like she was a joke.

"Do you understand?" Mrs. Ross raised her voice.

"Am I supposed to say, 'Yes, ma'am'?" Tiara snapped back. "Because if *that's* the response you're hoping for, you can just cut it. You can teach the class, though."

"Get out of my classroom, now!" Mrs. Ross yelled and pointed at the door, offended by the audacity of Tiara's words.

"Again?" Brandy said. "She didn't even do nothing!"

"It's cool, B," Tiara, who hadn't even gotten settled in her seat, stood up and said. "I know what this is really about." She threw her book bag over her shoulder and got in Mrs. Ross's face. "This bitch has had it out for me since the first day of school. What? You think I don't know what your problem with me is? You just mad because my father fucked you a long time ago, and then stopped returning your calls."

Mrs. Ross gasped and looked at Tiara like she wanted to smack the smug look from her pretty little face.

"Damn," Tiara taunted. "I hit that nerve, huh? My mother told me all about you. Why do you think that whenever you get the principal to call home about me, she doesn't do shit about it? Because she knows that you are just a bitter-ass woman who married a man you didn't love because the man you *wanted* married someone else. Get out of my way."

Tiara left Mrs. Ross standing there flabbergasted and moved past her. On her way out of the classroom, Ericka stuck her foot out in the aisle to trip Tiara. Tiara saw it just in time and shot Ericka a mean look.

"Bitch, don't get fucked up," Ericka sneered at her rival. "Your father isn't here to protect you right now."

Tiara finally had had enough of Ericka's smart mouth. She slapped her so hard that a red imprint immediately formed on her light-skinned cheek.

But Tiara didn't stop there. She threw her book bag off of her back and commenced to beating Ericka's face in. The whole class had gathered around the two girls, and Mrs. Ross scrambled to call security. A few of Ericka's friends saw her getting the life beat out of her and tried to intervene. One of them grabbed Tiara's hair while the other one tried to get a few hits in. But Brandy wasn't having any of that.

"Uh-uh! You whores aren't about to jump my bitch!" she yelled and got the girls off of Tiara.

It wasn't the first fight Tiara and Brandy had gotten into together, but they always shut things down. As usual, the two girls came out with a few scraps and bruises, but they always looked better than their opponents.

"Come on, let's go before those fuck boys show up," Tiara said and grabbed her book bag off the floor and Brandy's hand so that they could run out of the classroom together.

When they were out in the hallway, they decided to go to the usual spot where they cut class together, behind the stairwell in the very back of the school.

"Fuck!" Brandy said when they sat on the cold marble floor. "We weren't even in that class for fifteen minutes! My mom is going to kill me if the principal calls home again."

"Fuck it," Tiara said and unzipped her bag. "I'm rich. If I'm good, you will always be good. I promise that. This school stuff? I hate this shit. I can't wait to graduate. That shit just gave me the biggest attitude! They got me fucked up! Where's the trees at?"

She took out a pack of regular Cigarillo Swisher Sweets and removed one from the pack. She gutted it, and Brandy took out her weed and broke it down with her pink grinder.

"This is some good shit!" Brandy said. "I got it from my brother's stash."

"One day he's going to find out you've been stealing his weed," Tiara giggled.

"Well, for your sake, you better hope he doesn't. Here," she handed the broken-down weed to Tiara who put it in the brown wrap.

"I'm about to pearl this bitch; watch," she bragged.

She rolled the blunt so perfectly that a pothead would have envied it. The two girls took turns hitting the blunt and passing it.

"I'm glad you finally beat Ericka's ass," Brandy said. "I don't know why she thought that today was the right day to try you. Now she's in the nurse's office leaking!"

Tiara simply nodded her head. Her father had taught her how to fight, despite her mother's displeasure, when she was very young.

"I hate that bitch," Tiara said. "She's such a hater! Mrs. Ross too. My mom said she tried to trap my papi with a kid and . . . Well, you don't want to know what my mom did. Anyways, what did you say this shit was called again? 'Cause it's hitting the spot!"

"I didn't say," a high Brandy laughed. "But my brother said it's called Starburst or some shit like that. I told you it was some good shit!"

When they finished smoking, their eyes were low and bloodshot red. Knowing that they had more classes to go to, Brandy took out some eyedrops for them to use and some perfume spray.

"That's why you're my bitch," Tiara said and put two drops in each eye.

Just as they finished getting rid of the evidence and took one step from behind the stairwell, they saw one of the security guards of the school and the principal headed their way. Brandy hurriedly stuffed the grinder in her book bag, and the girls walked toward the two men headed their way.

"What's up, Principal Schroeder?" Brandy asked, her voice low and even.

Principal Schroeder was a man in his early forties with a head full of white hair. His face held many wrinkles from frowning at the students who frequented his office every day. That day he'd heard an urgent request for security being called for Tiara Rogers over his walkie-talkie. From the sounds of it, he knew he'd better be present for the pickup, but upon arriving to the class, he was informed that she and Brandy had fled. He searched the empty halls of the school for the two girls for more than thirty minutes before he finally found them.

"Hey, Principal Schroeder," Tiara greeted him in a stoner trance.

He looked back and forth between the two young women and noticed something was off about them. By the grins on their faces and the fact that the top of their eyelids were basically touching the bottom he knew they were high out of their minds. He breathed deeply and looked at the security officer standing slightly behind him.

"Take Brandy and escort her to her next class," he said. "Tiara, you come with me."

The girls went to protest, but one stern look from Principal Schroeder silenced both of them.

"See you at lunch, boo," Brandy said to Tiara before she was led off by the young security guard.

"Follow me," Principal Schroeder instructed Tiara.

She followed him, already knowing that he was about to take her to his office to have a one-on-one talk with her. It never failed. He either saw Tiara in his office every other week or once a month. Either way, it was far too much for his liking. He led her through the whole school until they got to his office. He opened the doors and walked through with Tiara close behind him. She smiled at the young secretaries who shook their heads when they saw her.

"Not again, Tiara," one of them by the name of Jen said.

She was the only one Tiara seemed to like in the whole office. Jen stared at Tiara with knowing eyes. Instead of responding with words, Tiara put her hands up and shrugged her shoulders. She was sure that Jen knew all about the fight. Tiara followed Principal Schroeder all the way back as he opened a glass door that led to his personal office. The office was spacious and neat. The walls were an off-white, and he had a flat-screen TV hanging from the ceiling. She looked around at all of his pictures on the walls.

That's when he went fishing. That's when his wife had their son. That's when he became principal.

Tiara recited the happenings of his photos as she sat down across from Principal Schroeder's desk. He stared into her eyes for a few moments as if waiting for her to speak first. When she didn't say a word, he sighed. Tiara's folder was already sitting on his desk, but instead of looking through it, he pushed it aside.

"Aren't you growing tired of seeing my office?"

"Never," Tiara said with a smile. "It's so interesting in here. Why would I ever get tired of seeing such a place?"

The principal heard the sarcasm in her voice and shook his head. "I think you behaved much better when your father had those bodyguards accompanying you to class," he said.

"I would be just fine if you would tell the teachers working here to watch their mouths," Tiara snapped back. "I would never get in trouble if people just talked to me right."

"You are a student. It is your responsibility to respect the teachers. And fighting is something that we just can't tolerate in this school!"

"So basically you're saying that it is OK for these teachers to talk to me crazy, but I can't defend myself verbally? And it is OK for a girl to try to trip me just as long as I don't hit her back? Why isn't she in the office too?"

"She is in the nurse's office, that's why."

"That's what that bitch gets," Tiara said, folding her arms with a smug expression on her face. She leaned back in her seat and looked the principal square in his eyes. "Because I'm sure that's the only form of discipline she's going to receive."

"Look, Tiara, I'm not sure what happened in that classroom today. All I know is that there are several witnesses saying that you took your frustration from Mrs. Ross out on Ericka."

"And how believable does that sound, Schroeder? Every time I come in this stupid office of yours you never believe me or anything that I say. So you know what? Forget it. Give me detention, in-school suspension, or whatever. I don't care."

Principal Schroeder thumbed through Tiara's file and saw all of the notes on this troubled kid. No form of discipline seemed to work with her, and whenever he called home, one of the Rogers's many housekeepers always answered the phone. He had tried to schedule conferences with her parents, but it was always her mother who came. And he had a feeling that Tiara and her mother didn't exactly see eye to eye when it came to certain things.

"It's to the point where I don't know what to do with you anymore, Tiara. And because your father made one of the most generous donations to the school, I am not in a position to suspend you or expel you."

Tiara translated that to, *"Your father put a lot of money into this school to pay us off, and we've already spent what he gave us. We can't do anything to you because we need more of your daddy's money. His money is more important to us than you."*

She shook her head. Nobody cared about her, and Principal Schroeder's next statement proved that.

"Just do me a favor and *try* to keep your nose clean for the next few months, OK? You have good enough grades, and you'll be ready to graduate soon. The sooner you can get your diploma, the sooner you can be out of this school and out of my balding head. Deal?"

"Whatever," she responded looking at the ground.

Suddenly there was a knock on the door to his office. Before he could answer, the secretary Jen opened it.

"I'm sorry to interrupt, sir, but I have a student here looking to get his class schedule. He's the new student."

"No problem. I was just done here," Principal Schroeder said. "Send him on in."

Tiara glanced up when she heard footsteps walking inside of the office. Her heart skipped a beat when they fell on the most handsome boy she had ever seen in her life. He was tall, muscular, and had the most gorgeous brown eyes in the universe. His hair was cut into a curly fade, and his skin was smooth and caramel. When he saw Tiara staring, he flashed her a perfect white smile, and his already high cheekbones rose even higher. His lips were luscious, and Tiara could not help but to stare. He was a pretty boy, but something about him read the complete opposite of that. He was dressed in the school uniform, but Tiara was drooling at how clear his muscles were defined through his blazer.

"Hey," he said to her.

"H-hey," Tiara swallowed her spit and waved a shaky hand.

"Jen, can you please get somebody to escort Tiara to her next class for me? I'm not sending her home today, but I also don't want any more fights breaking out in the hallways."

Jen winked at Tiara seeing the way she was looking at the new student. "Come on, Laila Ali," she said. "Let's get you back to class."

Tiara stood up, and the boy took her seat. She made like she was about to follow Jen, but right before she made it out of the office, she heard the boy's voice being directed at her again.

"Tiara?" he said, causing her to whip her head around. "I like that name."

"Thank you," she returned his smile. "What's your name?"

"Mario."

"Mario? Hmm . . . fits you. Well, I'll see you around, *Mario*."

"I do hope so."

Tiara hurried up and turned around before he could see her face turn beet red. Jen gave her a knowing look when she shut Principal Schroeder's door behind them. She called a security guard with her walkie-talkie to show Tiara to her next class. He showed up in no time, but before he left with Tiara, Jen grabbed her hand gently.

"Can this please be the last time I see you in this office?" she asked.

"I can't make any promises," Tiara told her with a sly smile. "But I can try to make my next visit not so soon."

Chapter 4

"Oh my gosh, girl, he was so fine!" Tiara was telling Brandy at lunch. "I have never seen anybody look so good except for on the Internet!"

Tiara had been waiting for her lunch period for what seemed like a whole year. When the bell finally rang in her AP Psychology class, she jetted out of the hallway to meet Brandy in the cafeteria. She spotted her instantly at the table they sat at every day with a few other girls, but Tiara didn't really care for them to know her business all like that. She sat down and spoke in a low, excited voice to her friend.

"Is he like, 'I'll ride his dick fine'?"

"Girl, he's 'I'll ride it, suck it, and swallow it' fine!"

"Stop it!" Brandy laughed and hit her friend on the arm. "Your virgin ass ain't swallowing nobody's kids!"

"Shiiiiiit!"

"So is he like here for the whole day? Like did he start school here already?" Brandy asked, happy that her friend finally had a crush.

She secretly had started to think that her friend was going the other way because she never gave any guys at their school a chance. She was truly excited to see her girl interested in a boy. She could see the giddiness in Tiara's eyes when she spoke about him and could only imagine what he looked like.

"Well, he was getting his class schedule, so I would assume that he does start today. He was also in his uniform."

"See! It was meant for you to beat the shit out of Ericka today! If you hadn't done that, then you wouldn't have had to go to the office, and you wouldn't have met the man of your dreams!"

Tiara burst out laughing. Brandy was really into that "destiny" mumbo jumbo, and she truly felt that everything happened for a reason. There was never anything left up to chance.

"Uh, man of my dreams?" Tiara raised her eyebrow still laughing. "I don't know about that, but he is sexy, though. Come on, there's enough girls here to hold the table down so let's get in the lunch line."

The two of them walked through all the students who had lunch that period and stopped when they got to one of the two lunch lines in the middle of the cafeteria. The two girls easily could have cut the whole line and nobody would say anything to them, but Tiara wasn't the type to abuse her power. Like always, the two of them got in the line wherever they fell in it.

"Tiara!"

Tiara heard a familiar voice call her name. She leaned back and looked up the line. What she saw made her smile. There was Mario waving at her and telling the two of them to come cut in line with him.

"Come on!" Tiara grabbed Brandy's hand, suddenly having a change of heart, and dragged her to the front of the line.

When Brandy's eyes laid on Mario, she understood exactly why her friend's mind was so gone. The boy was fine. Not just normal fine, like *GQ* magazine fine.

"Well, uh, hello," Brandy said and nudged Tiara with her shoulder giving her the silent "OK."

"Hey," Mario flashed them a charming smile. "You are?"

"Her best friend. My name is Brandy. I already know your name; no need to introduce yourself."

If looks could kill, then Tiara would have sent Brandy to an early death. Mario saw this and burst out laughing.

"You musta been talking about me then," he said to Tiara who made a face. "It's OK because I've been thinking about you too. I'm just glad that I could make a lasting impression."

He winked at a very embarrassed and speechless Tiara. Luckily for her, it was her turn to grab a tray and choose her lunch. Tiara wasn't a salad-eating girl. She chose a greasy hamburger, fries, and bought a lemonade with the tab her father had for her. When she reached the end of the line, she entered in her school ID and waited for the other two to join her.

"Do you have anywhere to sit?" Tiara asked Mario. "If not, you can sit with us."

She looked at the table they had just come from and saw that there were only two available seats. She looked at Brandy for help, knowing that this might be the only chance she got to make an impression on him. She'd already seen the way the other girls were eyeing him like a hawk, and she wanted to sink her claws in him first. Brandy was quick on her feet. She spotted an empty table not too far from where they were standing and pointed it out to them.

"Y'all go sit over there," Brandy said. "I'll go sit at our usual table and listen to these boring hoes talk about basic bitch shit by myself today. I'll see you after school, Ti Ti."

She gave Mario another look of approval before she took her tray of food back to the table she originated from. Tiara led the way to the table that Brandy pointed out, noticing all the curious looks being thrown her way. She even spotted Ericka at a table with all of her friends staring hatefully at Tiara as she sat down alone with Mario.

"So," Tiara started when they were situated across from each other, "what's up with you? Why did you transfer here when the school year is almost up? Are you a senior?"

Mario looked at Tiara with a blank face. "I mean, can I start my food before you start asking me all these questions?"

Tiara instantly knew that she had messed up.

"I-I'm sor—" but she stopped in mid-apology when Mario burst into a grin.

"Aye, I'm just fuckin' with you, girl."

"Childish ass!" Tiara grinned.

"But, nah, seriously, I'm not about to eat this nasty shit anyways," Mario said, making a face at his plate. "This shit looks deadly."

Tiara laughed so hard she almost choked on the piece of burger she had in her mouth.

"See? I'm cool on that!"

"You're so stupid!" Tiara said, still laughing.

"Never that," Mario licked his lips at her, causing her to blush. "But to answer your questions, my family moves a lot . . . Well, who I have left of my family."

He paused for a second, and Tiara wasn't sure, but she felt that he wanted to continue talking.

"What do you mean?"

"My mom was black, and my dad was Mexican. Neither one of them was really shit. But my dad's people? They were all about family. My aunt and uncle, well, they were the heart of my mixed-up-ass family. They worked odd jobs to make sure the entire family was a'ight, you know? My uncle finally landed this nice position where he was making a lot of money. Moved us all into this big house, and he was good to all of us. Shit was good for a long time . . . until somebody murdered him. That shit tore my family up, and even though I know my auntie is hurting the worst, she's trying to be the rock and hold everybody down."

"Where's your mother?"

"Probably in some crack house sucking some nigga's dick for her next high."

"I'm sorry, Mario. That's awful."

"Yea . . ." He had a distant look in his eyes.

"How did you end up in a private school?"

"Because I was getting into too many fights, so my aunt used the last of her savings to put me in this lovely place." He waved his hands around for emphasis. "She knew I wouldn't trick off her money because I respect her too much. She wants me to graduate and go to some white man's college."

"That's deep," Tiara said and then added shyly, "Well, I'm glad that this is the private school she decided to put you in."

"Me too . . . now."

Mario reached and grabbed Tiara's hand using his thumb to rub it. Thousands of butter-flies were released in her stomach, and the chills went from her neck to her toes.

OK . . . Is this what happens in the movies? Does it happen this fast? OK, Tiara . . . breathe. Don't trip out and be a weird bitch! she thought to herself and tried to force the butterflies out of her stomach.

"OK, now, what about you? So far, all I know is that you're the most beautiful girl in the school, and you like to fight bitches. I'm sure there is more to your storybook."

"Well, if you must know, yes, I did fight today. Lately, I've gotten into a lot of fights actually," she said, using her free hand to play with the food on her tray. "But the truth is that I hate to fight. I don't like causing other people physical pain. You have to really push me to that point. And at this school, I get tested a lot because of who my father is."

"Why? Does he own the school or something?"

"No, but he runs the streets of Texas," Tiara sighed.

"You say that like your dad is Blake Rogers or something," Mario laughed and looked at Tiara in hopes that she would laugh with him. When she didn't, his eyes widened. "Oh shit."

Out of instinct, he pulled his hand away from hers in a quickness, like he was touching property that was off-limits.

"See," Tiara said to him, shaking her head, "that's how all the guys treat me. Like I'm poisonous. Either that or they try to use me to get in good with my father."

Mario saw that he had genuinely hurt Tiara's feelings and replaced his hand on top of hers. He had heard through his own people that Blake Rogers's daughter attended the school he was going to be attending, but he didn't believe it. Least of all that she was the girl sitting in front of him. He'd also heard that his daughter was under constant supervised security. He looked around for Blake's hired hands but didn't see any. Tiara knew what he was looking for.

"You can't see them."

"See who?" Mario tried to act innocent.

"I know why you're looking around. There's no security people in here. My father decided to give me a little more space a few years ago. I got tired of being crowded all the time, so he's giving me more breathing room. I just want to be a normal girl."

"Nah, trust me. If you are who you say you are, them niggas are in here somewhere. Ain't no way a man like Blake Rogers would ever leave his daughter wide open like this. I'm sorry to put it to you like this, but you're something like a princess, shorty . . . There ain't nothing normal about that."

Tiara made a face at him. "Thanks. Thanks a lot."

His words made her think deeply. He made a lot of sense. Blake was a man with a lot of power and reach. If he didn't want his men seen, they wouldn't be seen. She groaned at the realization that he probably never really gave in to her request at all. She knew he had dozens of men on the outside to make sure nobody got into the school, and a few patrolled the hallways, but that was it.

"It's just for your protection, I'm sure," Mario said, seeing the sudden change in her mood.

"The type of dude in a high position like your father, there's gotta be hella niggas after his head. He gotta stay clear on all sides and protect his family, you feel me?"

"Sounds like you know a lot about the *underworld*," she teased.

"My uncle taught me a little something something. But, nah, for real, your father sounds like a smart man."

"He better be smart since all he seems to have time for is work these days," Tiara said with a little bit of salt in her voice.

"You and him aren't very close, I'm guessing."

"Nope."

"Well, don't take it to heart. I don't know what his life is like, but I can only assume that it's hectic as fuck."

"He shouldn't have had a kid then."

"Ooookay," Mario said, realizing his words hadn't really helped any.

"I'm sorry," Tiara knew she was targeting her bitterness at the wrong person. "I didn't mean to sound like a bitch."

At that moment the bell rang, signaling that their lunch period was now over. Mario grabbed both of their trays and took them to the trash can.

Great! You just blew your chance with him! Tiara thought to herself standing to her feet.

Mario came back to the table and grabbed his book bag. "I have a way you can make it up to me," he said, interrupting her negative thoughts. "Go out with me this weekend? To dinner on Saturday. Maybe we can go to a movie or somethin'?"

"That's perfect!" Tiara said a little too fast. "I mean, uhh, let me check my schedule, and I'll get back to you. Here, take my number."

She hurried up and gave him her number. Then she looked over his shoulder and saw Brandy standing at one of the cafeteria exits looking impatient. She grinned, knowing that Brandy was dying to know what had transpired during their lunch period. She told Mario she would see him later and walked away without looking back. When she reached Brandy, the two girls linked arms and bustled their way through the mounds of students in the hallway.

"Soooo?" Brandy shook her arm a little bit. "You're killin' me, Smalls!"

"I like him," Tiara said with a dreamy look on her face. "I like him a lot."

Tiara went to Brandy's house that day after school to go over their homework from that day. She sent a quick text to her mother when her driver drove her and Brandy away from the school. When they arrived at Brandy's house, Tiara said a quick hello to her mother and kissed Brandy's little brother Lawrence on his forehead. Brandy led the way to her bedroom and once there, both girls threw their book bags to the side.

"Well, I guess they haven't called home yet," Brandy said. "My mom is being nice."

"They probably already called my house," Tiara said. "I doubt Stephanie told my mom, though. You know she doesn't give a fuck about what I do. There would be no point."

"That's crazy," Brandy said. "Anyways, back to *Mariooooo*."

The singsong voice she used made Tiara roll her eyes. "What about him?" Tiara tried to sound nonchalant.

"Bitch, now it's 'what about him,' when you were just hella geeked at the school behind his ass!"

"Nah, I'm just kidding," Tiara said, grinning. "He's just so cool. I don't know, there is just something about him that I like. He's not like the other guys who I thought liked me. They all just tried to use me to get on with my papi's business. Mario didn't even care that I'm Blake Rogers's daughter. I was just Tiara today at the lunch table, and you don't know how good that felt, Brandy."

"Well, shit," Brandy winked. "You're always just Tiara to me. You don't get special treatment, ho!"

"Shut up," Tiara said, smiling dreamily. "I'm trying to be serious with you!"

At that moment, she felt her smartphone vibrate in her pocket. When she checked the name, she squealed excitedly and used her butt to bounce up and down on Brandy's bed.

"It's him!"

"What'd he say?"

"Ummm," Tiara checked the message. "He said, 'wassup, ma?' Ahhh! What should I say? What should I say? I don't want to sound too geeked. Should I wait like ten minutes before texting back?"

Brandy looked at Tiara like she was an alien and burst out laughing.

"Brandyyyyy!" Tiara poked her lip out and looked desperately to her friend for help. She had never really talked to a boy that she liked so much, and she didn't want to mess it up by saying the wrong thing.

"Okay okay okay," Brandy said. "Just ask him about how his day was. That's always a good conversation starter, and then after that, just let it flow naturally, chica."

"OK," Tiara said, sending the text and while she was sending it, Brandy was eyeing her.

"Ti Ti," Brandy told her, "before you get that pretty head wrapped up in a boy, just remember the rules to the game."

Tiara raised an eyebrow and cocked her head to the side. "Rules? What rules?"

"Rule number one is to never give too much too soon. Rule number two is to never lose yourself behind any man. And rule number three is to always remember that you are beautiful and young. The guy you meet now most likely isn't who you're going to marry, so there isn't really a point in trying to get in too deep."

"You mean fall in love?"

"Exactly."

"OK, Confucius," Tiara said sarcastically.

"I'm being serious, T!" Brandy laughed. "For real, just follow those rules and I promise you will be saved from a world of heartbreak."

"Well, I'm a firm believer of following whatever path you're on at the moment."

"Bitch, you just made that shit up."

"So?" Tiara laughed.

Tiara stayed over at Brandy's house for the next few hours. She texted with Mario on and off, and the girls finished their homework. She knew that by having her homework already done by the time she got home, it would save her from receiving too bad of a verbal lashing from Stephanie. Tiara pictured Stephanie sitting on her bed waiting for her to walk through the bedroom doors just *ready* to dig in. She knew her mother wouldn't be too upset about what happened with the teacher, but she'd be furious about her fight with Ericka. When it was time for them to say good-bye, the two girls hugged each other tightly like they would never see each other again.

"See you at school!" Brandy waved to Tiara before her driver took off.

Tiara waved back out of the window and then rolled it up. She had just gotten comfortable in her seat when her phone vibrated again. She grinned when she read the message on her screen.

There's just something about you. I don't know what it is, but I can't get you out of my mind. Call me when you get home.

Tiara quickly sent him an "OK" text and held the phone to her chest with her eyes closed. She silently willed for Thomas to drive faster so that she could hurry up and call him. She couldn't wait to hear his voice. The whole ride she tried to think of different topics to talk about so that they wouldn't just be sitting on the phone listening to each other breathing.

Tiara barely paid attention to the scenery that the car passed by on the way, but when they finally pulled up, she had never been so grateful to see the gates of their home. That had felt like the longest car ride she'd ever been on.

"Thank you!" Tiara called to Thomas and hopped out of the vehicle before it was all the way in park.

Thomas sputtered something to her about her safety, but she didn't hear him. She'd already slammed the door shut. Tiara ran into the house and up the stairs so that she could confine herself in her bedroom. She looked over the stair railing back to the first floor and saw that her mother was in the living room watching one of her sitcoms. She didn't even acknowledge the fact that Tiara was home. Normally this wouldn't have surprised Tiara, but since she was expecting a verbal lashing from Cat, she found it a bit strange. However, Tiara didn't care enough to dwell on it. At this moment, she only had one thing on her mind.

When she reached her room, she took her phone out preparing to dial Mario's number, but a throat being cleared interrupted her in mid-button press. She turned her head—and there was her father sitting calmly with his legs crossed on her bed. His eyes went straight to the red lipstick on her lips, and she immediately remembered that her hair had been in a ponytail that morning, not flowing loose off of her shoulders like now.

Tiara was frozen as she watched her father study her and wished she could turn and run out of the room. She could already tell just by looking at the expression on his face that she was in trouble. It was too late to purse her lips to hide the redness on them or to tuck her hair behind her ears. She was stuck like Chuck, and there was nothing she could do about it.

"So, what's this I hear about a fight at school? And before you start talking, go to your bathroom and wipe that mess off of your mouth."

Tiara didn't even think to argue. She just did as she was told. When she came back, she stood in front of him and put her head down.

"If you were bold enough to sneak and do it, then you must have known there would be a chance that you would be caught," Blake's voice was venomous. "Put your head up and look me in my eyes since you can defy me behind my back."

"Yes, sir," she said and looked him in his eyes.

"What happened at school today?"

"This girl tried to trip me, and I had to handle my business. I've been ignoring her all year because I didn't really want to fight her. But at the end of the day, I ain't no punk. I had enough of her, and she needed to learn her lesson."

Blake nodded his head. There was no lesson that he could teach there because she had done what he would've done. In this moment, Blake realized she was indeed her father's daughter. He hadn't raised her to be a doormat.

"OK. Next topic. When you walked in this room, you looked nothing like the daughter that was birthed for me. You are a princess, not a whore."

Tiara looked genuinely hurt by his words, but he was not moved. She stood before him with disheveled hair and an open blouse. He saw no difference between her and the hoes his young soldiers hit and quit on a daily basis. Her appearance mirrored that of a woman that had just gotten fucked by the crew and sent home in an Uber.

"Daddy, why would you say that to me?"

"Because that is what you look like. Got your blouse all open, hair all messy. Why the fuck would you ever think that it was OK to walk into my house looking like you just got screwed by three different men? If a nigga saw you in the streets, he wouldn't respect you. Do you know why? Because you look easy. An easy target.

I couldn't even blame him for not respecting Blake Rogers's daughter. Shit, *I* don't even recognize you."

Tears formed in her eyes because he had never before said anything like that to her. Blake realized then that maybe he had been so strict on her that she had become one of those kids that felt she had to sneak to do everything. Cat often watched those shows that showed the outlandish things that teenage kids did behind their parents' backs. His mind began to wander off reflecting on his parenting over the last couple of years. Stephanie's words eerily rang in his head as he stared at his daughter, wondering if he knew her as well as he thought he did. He also began to wonder about all of the things that Tiara might have been doing behind his back.

"You out here fucking, Tiara?"

"No, Daddy, I promise. I'm still a virgin," she said with sincerity in her voice.

"Aw . . . So you just out here trying to get these little niggas' attention and get their dicks hard, huh?"

"No, sir."

"So what is it then? Why do you feel the need to look like a ho?"

"I'm not a ho. This is how the other girls at school dress."

Blake sighed and shook his head at his daughter. He wanted to wring her neck but realized that it was just as much his fault as it was hers. Cat's too. He loved his wife very much, but he'd be lying if he said she was Mrs. Huxtable. She was as beautiful as they came, but her appearance was that of a sexy vixen. He was silent for a minute before he stood up and his full six-foot-two figure loomed over her. He was dressed comfortably in Ralph Lauren pajamas with matching house slippers. His hair was neatly lined up, and he was so handsome that you didn't pay attention to the dew gray he had sprouting in the front. He was giving Barack Obama a run for his money.

"Come on," he said and stepped around her. "Come to the basement with me."

He led the way to their spacious basement, and as she walked slightly to his right, he saw her hurry to button up her shirt. Growing up, Blake didn't have much at all, and he always promised himself that if he was going to do it, he was going to do it big. His house was the visual proof of that, and his basement was his joy. It was what he called the ultimate man cave. He had a theater that fit thirty, a bar with a connected dance floor, a lounge section, and to top it all off, a metal door that led to his own personal gun range. When he was home, he was most likely in his basement because it was his personal escape from his everyday life. When he was in the basement, he felt like whatever was going on in his life was outside of the basement doors. In his man cave, he had peace and tranquility.

"What are you doing?" Tiara asked when, instead of taking her to one of the lounge chairs, he went to the console room instead.

He opened the small door that controlled the power in the house, or so Tiara thought. Instead of switches that controlled the entire house's fuses and lights, however, there was a keypad behind the door. He entered a code that she recognized as her birthday, and she heard a click and a soft hum. She was thrown completely for a loop when the entire wall opened up. She stepped closer to it and examined it, seeing that it wasn't a wall at all. It was a metal door.

"I never knew this was down here," Tiara said in awe when he pushed it all the way open revealing not only a gun range, but an entire artillery room.

"Every kingpin has an artillery room," he said, stepping through the door. "Go on, pick up a gun."

"How am I supposed to know which one to pick?" Tiara asked, walking into the room.

The walls were white, and on all of them were weapons. From handguns to automatics. From knives to explosives. She wanted to say she was shocked, but she'd heard all of the stories about her father just like everybody else. The only thing was, now, she knew they were true.

"When you put the right one in your hand, you'll know. Go ahead. You said you wanted to learn to shoot, right? Let's do it."

She trailed the wall until finally she reached and grabbed one.

"Put that Desert Eagle down. You gon' hurt yourself."

Tiara grinned and glanced behind her at her father staring at her with a raised eyebrow.

"You said to grab what I wanted. This one is pretty!"

"You don't shoot a gun because it's pretty." Blake shook his head at her. "That thing has power, too much power for you. We can work our way up to it in time, though."

She put the gun back and tried again with a gun right next to it. It was black and gray and smooth to the touch. It wasn't heavy at all and was small enough to fit in one of her designer tote bags if she wanted. She looked back at her dad to get his approval, and he nodded his head.

"That's a Glock 19. Made of polymer, not metal. Come get a clip and cover your ears up."

He taught her how to load the gun, take it on and off safety, and finally how to aim.

"Point, hold it firm, and shoot. Imagine that you're the bullet. You hate when people waste your time, right? So don't waste a bullet."

He allowed her to step into the lane and aim at one of the still posts at the end of the lane. They all had pictures of people on them, and he thought that might intimidate her. But to his surprise, she began firing with no hesitation. She grunted every time she pulled the trigger, and her brow wrinkled like she was focusing harder than she'd ever focused in her life. It was apparent that she was letting off some kind of steam. He was pleased to see that she had taken his advice. Every bullet had met its target. She would need more practice on precise aim, but this had been a great start.

"Good job. The only thing is you got more stomachs and arms than foreheads. If you want your enemy to live and come back with a vengeance, those are the perfect places to shoot. But understand that if you ever have to brandish your gun, you better use it lethally. Now, watch me."

He went to the wall and grabbed his Sig Sauer P229 and loaded it with ease. He took a few steps to the lane where he pressed a button, and the posts all became moving targets.

Bot! Bot! Bot! Bot! Bot! Bot!

Tiara watched her dad shoot and not only hit all of the targets, but she noticed that every bullet hole found a home in the heads of the posts. Blake reloaded and aimed again. She knew why he'd made her put on the earplugs. Between the gun going off and the bullets hitting their mark, it was very loud. She observed that he did not have anything on his ears, however.

After all of these years he's gotta be used to this noise, she thought.

When he finally drew back, he was breathing hard. Not from being exhausted, but because he too needed to let off some steam. He placed his gun down and took the one from Tiara's hand.

"I think it's safe to say your first lesson was a success. Now, come sit down and talk to your old man."

Taking her out from the gun range and to the bar, he pulled out a stool for her to sit down on. He went behind the bar and pulled out a glass and a bottle of scotch. Pouring himself a shot, he swiveled it around in the cup trying to think of the right words to say.

"I haven't been the best father to you, Tiara, but I can honestly say I have always wanted the best for you. And because of that, I am who I am in Dallas. Because of that, the people in

Houston stand up straight when I pass them. And because of that, it has caused me to be home less than I should. But let me tell you something, little girl. You are my daughter, and that may not mean much to you, but to the outside looking in, it means everything. You have eyes on you that you may not even know exist. I can't have you out here looking like you are not the child of a king."

"So it's all about your image?"

"No. There's a lot more to it than just image." Blake took a deep breath and released it slowly, "It's about looking and being strong. The way you're carrying yourself out there right now, Tiara, the way you're dressing and sneaking around, you look weak, Tiara. I always thought that shielding you from the life that I live would do you some good, but instead, it has made you green. No, not green. Dumb and naive."

"Daddy, all I did was put on a little lipstick and unbutton my shirt a little."

"It's not that simple, Tiara!" Her father's thundering voice made her jump and take a step back from him, "I keep a pack of wolves around me at all times! Tiara, every man knows the way to a man's heart is through his wife or children. And the same wolves that I have running for me are the same ones that go for the women and children of my enemies! Those enemies have wolves of their own, and with you walking around acting and dressing the way that you are, they're gonna smell you from a mile away."

His voice was crisp, and Tiara made a mental note of not saying anything else that would upset him.

"Do you think I have an artillery room in my home for just show? Do you think I have hired hands with you at all times just because? No! I do that because of the blood that is on my hands due to providing you the life that people dream of! And because of that, I need to keep those around me protected."

"I didn't ask for this."

"Because you didn't have to!" Blake barked. "Because of all that I have done, you, you and your children . . . and your children's children will be set for eternity. Everything that I have done? I would do it all over again. Hell's fury does not scare me if I have paved the way to heaven for all of you. Now, don't you ever, *ever* come into my home, a home that I built from the ground up, the way you did today. And let this be the last time that I have to talk to you about fighting some floozy little bitch in school that ain't worth your time. You are the daughter of a king, and you will conduct yourself as such. Do you understand me?"

Tiara felt the tears streaming down her face, and she swallowed the lump in her throat. She nodded her head, unable to speak. Blake downed the last of the scotch that was in his cup and placed the glass on the bar. He came back from around it and sat in the stool beside his daughter. Running his fingers through her hair, he placed a kiss on her forehead.

"The last thing I want to do is hurt you, Tiara. When I am gone, rightfully, you will have the choice to take my place, given that you perfect your aim. Or you can choose to follow your own path. You said you did things because other girls are doing them, but I need you to understand that you were born better than them. Because you have my blood in your veins, you have already been set apart from everyone. You are cut from a different cloth, and you don't need to wear lipstick or show off your body to keep up with the hussies out there. As long as you wake up every morning, you already won the race."

He opened his arms, and within seconds, Tiara leaned into his broad chest. He hugged her tightly to him, and in that moment, he wished she could stay in his arms, in that spot with him forever.

Chapter 5

Blake Rogers sat in a plush white seat on his private jet as it made its way to Miami. He had some major business to wrap up there, but for some reason, his mind was on everything *but* business. He thought about the conversation that he had with his wife right before he left. His words had been harsh, and even though he wished he could take them back, he knew they needed to be said. After Tiara's outburst, Cat sat down at the table with tears falling from her eyes. She had looked at Blake and shook her head.

"I can't believe she talks to me that way!"

"Why not?" Blake said. "She's completely right."

Cat was even more surprised to hear those words from her own husband. She choked on her spit when she tried to prevent her sob from coming out.

"How can you agree with her? I have done my best to raise that girl!"

"No, you haven't. Neither one of us has." Blake was looking at his paper, but his eyes didn't focus on any of the words. "We tried, but not hard enough. And now whenever we try to mend the relationship with her, we aren't consistent. We give her so much and then take it away from her in a heartbeat. We expect her to act and behave a certain way, but we haven't taken the time to teach her. I know I haven't, and you damn sure haven't either."

Cat was silently listening to her husband, but she still did not agree with his words. When he paused, she wiped her tears away and spoke again.

"I just feel that she has everything she has ever wanted, and she is simply ungrateful. I'm tired. I'm tired of getting calls from that school of hers. I'm tired of going up there and meeting with the principal!"

"What I don't understand, my love," Blake disregarded everything Cat had just said, "is that you have been a stay-at-home mom and wife for almost eighteen years. Why isn't your relationship with her better? I'm not making any excuses for myself, but the fact of the matter is that you focus more on yourself than your own child. I do what I have to do to keep money in our accounts and to ensure that we will never have to need for anything. What do *you* do?" He waited for some type of response from his wife, and when he didn't get one, he continued to speak.

"I knew when I married you that you were not the type to take any part in my business ventures, and that is fine. You can keep your hands clean. But what I did not know was that even after you had a child that you would continue to put yourself first. Why is it that the help knows our child more than you do, when you should be with her as much as them? I'm not saying it is OK for Tiara to speak to you out of turn, and I will handle that, but do you really blame her for feeling the way that she does?"

Cat was trying to find words to respond with when she was saved by a ringing cell phone. The couple soon realized it was Blake's phone. When he answered it, he was informed that his car was ready to drive him to his jet.

"Babe, I have to go. We can finish this conversation when I get back," he said to his wife. "While I'm gone, think on what I have just said to you. I love you."

He kissed her on her forehead and made his exit.

While on his flight, he tried to get some much-needed rest, but he couldn't stop thinking about the situation with his wife and daughter. Here he was, the most powerful kingpin in his state. He ruled the streets with an iron fist, and he kept his business and his soldiers on such a tight ship that no one would dare question or try to go against him. For someone who had such a strong control over things, who would have guessed that he wouldn't be able to keep his own family in order. He knew he needed to make drastic moves to get things together on the home front, or else he feared that he would lose his daughter forever.

"Blake!"

Blake snapped out of his thoughts and turned his attention toward Vincent who had accompanied him on the trip.

"That's the third time I called your name."

"I'm sorry," Blake said, motioning for his flight attendant to come and poor him a shot of tequila. "I was deep in thought."

"Yeah, I could tell," Vincent said, studying his older cousin. The way his forehead was scrunched up, Vincent could tell something was really bothering him. "Anything you want to talk about?"

"Ah," Blake said and threw the shot back, "it's just Tiara."

"Boys?"

"Hell, no. I'll shoot any motherfucker she brings through the door."

"Believe me," Vincent said. "I know. But she's almost eighteen. It's about that time for her to start getting all googly-eyed and mushy over boys."

"Thank you for your honesty," Blake said sarcastically.

"My bad, man. I was just trying to get you to crack a smile," Vincent said, realizing his friend was not in a joking mood. "What's going on with Tiara?"

"She's fighting in school, and I caught her wearing makeup and dressed like the rest of them little hoes we be seeing in the streets," Blake said as he asked for another drink to be served, "I've tried talking with her, but I don't know if my words have gotten through to her at all."

Vincent took a moment to absorb what Blake had just expressed to him. He had been around Tiara a few times and noticed how different she was from the girl he had once known. She had grown up and became her own person, which wasn't necessarily a bad thing. What was concerning for him was how withdrawn she had become. She never seemed to want to talk with anyone in the house, and when he was around her, he would get a weird vibe from her. Like as if she was up to something. With a father as busy as Blake, it was the mother's job to keep the child well rounded, and Vincent had learned a long time ago that Cat wasn't willing or even trying to do anything with Tiara. Vincent had warned Blake about marrying a woman like Cat. She was selfish and didn't know the first thing about connecting to a child.

"I guess I could have seen that coming," Vincent said, shaking his head. "She's just a teenager who needs some guidance, that's all. If this deal goes without a hitch, you'll be able to take a whole year off to dedicate to being a father."

"Not if she goes to college," Blake said sadly.

"College?" Vincent scoffed. "What does she need a degree for when she can be a CEO at age eighteen? We're Rogers. We make our own way. Fuck a degree."

Blake laughed and shook his finger at his cousin. "You're a crazy fool, man," he said. "I want her to have an education. Who knows, she might go into something in the legal field. If that's the case, I'm going to be firing Bernard. That nigga getting too old for this shit."

He spoke of his lawyer, and the two men shared a hearty laugh.

"Just don't stress yourself out too much," Vincent said. "At times like this, I'm glad my daughter is only five years old."

Blake smiled at the mention of his beautiful little cousin Mia. Just like Tiara was the spitting image of him, Mia was the spitting image of her father. Suddenly, regret filled his gut as he remembered that Mia's existence almost never took place. If he had killed Vincent that night, he would have never had the joy of becoming a father.

"Do you truly forgive me for that night?" Blake asked Vincent, looking straight into his eyes.

"You ask me this question at least twice a year." Vincent leaned forward in his seat across from Blake. "*Sí*, I do. All of my bones healed, and I am alive and kicking it. If the roles would have been switched, I would have done the exact same thing." He extended his hand. "By shaking my hand now, you are promising to never bring that shit up again. My knee gets this weird feeling whenever you make me think back to that day. You have a mean swing; always have since we were kids!"

After the two men shook hands, the pilot announced that they had arrived and to put their seat belts back on to prepare for the landing.

"If you close this deal, Blake, you're going to change the heroin game in both Texas *and* Florida."

"*If* I close the deal?" Blake said, fixing his suit and tie. "I don't travel *anywhere* unless it's a sure thing. The deal has already closed, and I haven't even shown up or showed my face yet."

Blake touched his hip to feel the gun there. He pulled it from his waist and checked the clip.

"How many did you send before us?"

"A whole fleet."

"Good," Blake said. "Rodriguez isn't going to know what hit him. I think that the contract will be signed within the hour."

"You're a crazy motherfucker, man," Vincent said, checking his own gun.

"If you've noticed, all the greats have been crazy motherfuckers," Blake said. "After today, I'll be on that list."

Chapter 6

The rest of the week Tiara shocked the hell out of Stephanie. Whenever she went in to wake her up in the morning, not only was she already awake, she was dressed too. Tiara didn't care about hiding the way she really wore her hair from her father and mother anymore. She took her time in the morning with her wand curls and refused to put it in a ponytail. She wanted to be seemingly flawless when she showed her face at school. She and Mario had been spending a lot of time together. They texted each other throughout the school day, and when they both got home from school, they talked on the phone all night. She found out that they had so much in common, and she loved the fact that he was a deep thinker. He had dreams of one day becoming a famous architect.

When they were at school, they met up in-between class periods to talk to each other since Tiara hadn't yet figured out a way to get out of the house to see him outside of school. She was still working on how she was going to make it to their date on Saturday. The only way she could think of was to lie and tell her parents that she was going to Brandy's house for the weekend, but knowing her father, he would still send like two men with her for safety. She could try to sneak out Brandy's window, but she'd get caught faster than a cheater who forgot to delete their text messages.

As Saturday grew nearer, she finally came to terms with the fact that she would just have to flat-out tell her parents that she had a date. There was no getting around it if she wanted to go.

On Friday after she got ready for school, she took a deep breath before she went downstairs to speak to her parents. Stephanie came and kissed her on the cheek. Tiara had already told her about her dilemma, and she said she would be there for moral support.

"*Ay probrecita*," Stephanie said and gripped Tiara's shoulders, "it won't be so bad. Come on, you have to go now or you'll be late for school. You've been making me so proud, by the way. I should have known there was a boy involved."

Tiara began the walk of death down the stairs—not really, but that was what it felt like. Whenever she was about to stop walking, Stephanie gave her a small push. They walked in the direction of Tiara's parents' voices which were, of course, located in the kitchen.

"My daughter!" Blake said, greeting her. "Sit down; have some breakfast before you have to leave."

He saw Stephanie behind Tiara, but he didn't say anything about it. When she didn't sit down, Blake looked up again.

"I'm not hungry, Daddy," Tiara said and then looked back at Stephanie who did a "shooing" motion with her hands, urging Tiara to continue. "I have something I want to ask you."

Cat stopped eating her oatmeal and tuned into the conversation at hand. Blake set his paper aside and gave Tiara his undivided attention.

"What is on your mind, Princess?"

"You see, uh . . . I . . ." Tiara searched for the words. She couldn't believe that she didn't practice that part at all. Finally, she just said forget it and spit it out. "There is this boy at school who I like, and he seems to like me just as much back. His name is Mario, and he asked me to go on a date with him on Saturday. I told him that I would love to go, but I would have to ask you first. Can I please go?"

Blake looked at Tiara as if he had never before seen her a day in his life. He was at a loss for words because that was definitely the last thing he expected her to say. He had done good and lucked out for almost four years, but now, there he was with the inevitable staring him in the face. He should have known something was up by the way Tiara carried herself lately. He was forced to see her as a beautiful young lady and not as his baby girl. Still, he would try to prolong it for as long as he could.

"What about our agreement, Tiara?" he said evenly.

"What about it, Daddy?" Tiara asked. "It's not like I'm about to have sex with him; it's just dinner. I really want to go, Daddy. Please?"

Tiara couldn't remember the last time she begged anyone for anything, especially her father, and that should have showed him that she really wanted to go.

"I will not allow it," Blake said and then picked up his paper again. "Tell him that I said no."

"What?" Tiara asked incredulously. "Why?"

She knew he might say no, but not just flat-out like that. He didn't even have a reason.

"Because I said so," Blake said. "It is not up for debate. That boy isn't looking at you for you. He's looking to get into your pants or to get in good with me. Like they always do."

"He's not like that, Daddy! Just give him a chance," Tiara tried one more time. She then looked to Cat for help, but she shook her head. "I don't understand what is the point of having a kid when you don't let me do anything! You don't even have a real reason to not let me go, and, Mom, you are just going based off of what *he* says because I don't think you have a mind of your own. You're just trying to control me, and it's not fair to me. If I can't go, I won't have anything to say to you this weekend, so don't come knocking on my door!"

Tiara ran out of the kitchen to the waiting car that was to take her to school. Stephanie put her hand on her hip and looked at Blake like he had shit on his face. Blake looked at her venomously, daring her to speak out of turn. Stephanie was bold enough to step out of line and talk crazy to Cat, but she would never have enough guts to do the same to Blake. Instead, she bit her tongue, taking her leave and went to find some work to do. She wanted to busy herself to keep Tiara's hurt voice off of her for the rest of the day.

"He said no," Tiara told Mario the second she saw him in the hallway. "He didn't even care to hear me out. He just said no."

Mario used his hand to gently brush against Tiara's cheek. "It's OK, beautiful. I will see you this weekend one way or another."

There was something about the determination in his voice that made her want to draw closer to him. He was looking extra fine that day too. She placed her hands on his chest, forcing Mario to lean against a locker behind him, and she leaned on him. She moved her hands so that her breasts could press into his chest as she gazed up into his sexy eyes.

"But how?" she asked.

Instead of answering, Mario leaned down and kissed her softly, something they had been doing quite often lately. Tiara slipped her tongue in his mouth, and she felt one of his hands put pressure on the small of her back while the other cupped her chin. It was Tiara who finally broke the kiss because she had to come up for air. She was sure she was about to faint because everything about Mario was so perfect. She felt her clit throbbing and wished they were somewhere more private so she could ask him to kiss her down there too. She had to see him on Saturday, even if it meant going against her father's wishes.

"I'm going to sneak out." It was like a lightbulb was flashing in Tiara's head. "I'm going to sneak out on Saturday night! I'm going to give you my address, and I want you to wait outside the gate for me to come out at midnight, OK?"

Mario looked down at Tiara trying to read her face. At first, he thought she was joking, but seeing the seriousness in her expression, he knew she wasn't.

"Are you sure that's the best idea? I'm sure all he needs to do is meet me and he will be open to me dating his daughter."

"You don't know my father. He would rather hang himself on a fishing hook and be thrown to the sharks than to see me grow up and have a boyfriend."

"Boyfriend?" Mario smiled slyly down at Tiara.

"W-well, you know what I mean," she said.

"Yeah, I do," Mario said and kissed her again. "It means we are officially together now. Nobody can stop this, not even your father."

The bell that signaled them being almost tardy sounded, and all of the students surrounding them began to put a pep in their steps.

"I better get going too," she said to Mario biting his lip sexily. "I'll see you at lunch?"

"I have to leave early today," Mario told her. "But I will call you tonight, and we can talk more about tomorrow night, OK?"

"OK."

***

"You sure this is the house, bro?"

Mario looked in the backseat at his friend Demetrius and nodded his head.

"Yea. This is the house."

"A'ight, let's get it then."

Four young men, including Mario, sat in his car a few houses down from their mark. The other three were Demetrius, Lee, and Rex. They all wore black hoodies and jeans. Word on the street was the side bitch of a big-time hustler had moved into a block not too far away from theirs. She was the type of chick that ran her mouth too much. She had bragged to the wrong person about the fact that her boo dropped all of his money off at her house until he could find a way to clean it. The person she told happened to be Demetrius's girlfriend.

"Thank God for beauty salons," Demetrius grinned and pulled down the mask on his face.

The boys in the car all followed suit. Lee's dreads hung out of his mask, which was a good thing because he and Rex were the same body build. Now Mario would be able to tell them apart. They made sure their guns were loaded and that their safeties were off before they got out of the car ducking down.

Cloaked by the darkness of the night, the boys made their way effortlessly to the house.

Mario hoped there was at least fifty stacks in the home so that way he would be able to sit on it for a while. After his uncle was killed, things had been tight in his house. His aunt Jay deserved so much. She took him in without question when his mother dropped him off with nothing but a diaper on. He owed her his life, literally, and every day, it seemed that she got another wrinkle on her beautiful face from all the stress she was under. Lately, he'd been using the skills that his uncle had taught him to break and enter homes. He was just doing what he had to do to survive.

The game plan was always the same. Demetrius would kick down the door, and the rest of them would plow through the door waving their guns until they got what they came for. Usually, they got in and out without anybody getting hurt, but that night would prove to be completely different. Demetrius had been scoping out the house, and he said that there would be nobody home at the time of the break-in. When they reached the door, Mario nodded his head at Demetrius, giving the silent order to kick the door down.

Boom!

"Go!"

They all ran through the open door with their guns in front of their bodies. The door led right into the living room of the two-story house. The lights were all off on the lower level.

"Grab anything that looks valuable," Mario instructed. "But look for the money first."

They all split up. He and Demetrius went upstairs while the other two, Lee and Rex, stayed on the lower level. Upstairs were two bedrooms.

"If I were a dumb bitch, where would I put a boatload of money?" Demetrius asked out loud, making Mario laugh.

"The master bedroom," they answered in unison.

They ran to the master bedroom at the end of the hall and began to ransack it. Demetrius checked under the bed and pulled all of the drawers out of the dressers while Mario hit the closet. He opened all of her shoe boxes and moved all of her clothes to the side.

"Man! It ain't in here. Let's check the basement."

Just when Mario was about to agree and turn to step out of the walk-in closet, a black bag in the corner of the overhead shelf caught his eyes. With his heart beating quickly, he reached up and grabbed the short straps on the bag.

"Bro!" Mario called out when he opened the bag.

"What, nigga? I'm about to go check the other room."

"You might not have to." Mario stepped out of the closet with a grin on his face.

He held up a stack of hundred-dollar bills.

"Hell, yeah!" Demetrius cheered and peeked into the bag. "That looks like way more than fifty Gs."

"On God!"

"It's lit! Now, let's get them other two niggas and get the fuck up outta here!"

Mario flicked off the light in the room, following after Demetrius when he heard something that made his blood run cold.

"Yo, what the fuck, Tesha!"

It was a voice that Mario didn't recognize, but he knew that Tesha was the owner of the house they were in.

"Oh my God, Ro!" a woman's voice screamed. "Somebody broke into my house!"

Mario stepped quietly to the corner of the wall where the staircase started. He slowly peered around it and down the steps. Still standing in the doorway was a big buff man and a petite woman. He was glaring at her like he wanted to kill her.

"Bitch, fuck yo' house. Where the fuck is my money?"

"R-Ro! I didn't, I swear I didn't set this up!"

Mario watched Ro backhand her so hard her head jerked to the side.

"Bitch, I said, *where* is my money?"

"I-it's in my room. In the closet!"

Ro pulled out two pistols from his waist and started toward the stairs. Mario ducked back around the corner and looked at Demetrius.

"Shit!" he whispered and backed away from the staircase repositioning the bag on his shoulder. "What do we do?"

"We gon' have to kill this nigga."

"We didn't wear gloves!"

"Shit!"

They looked around for a getaway, but it turned out that they wouldn't need one.

"Aye! There ain't nothing downstairs in the basement!" Rex yelled, coming back upstairs from the basement.

"Yeah, it gotta be upstairs!"

Lee would never know how he saved Mario and Demetrius's lives because he paid for them with his own.

Bot! Bot! Bot!

Mario peeked around the corner just in time to see Ro place a bullet neatly in the middle of Lee's forehead.

"Shit!" Rex yelled and tried to aim his own gun while attempting to go back into the basement.

Ro was firing shots, and Rex was ducking down and firing back. Soon, they were out of Mario's sight, and all he could hear was gunshots in the basement.

"Go go go!" Demetrius urged, but he didn't have to tell Mario twice. He was already halfway down the stairs.

Tesha almost had a heart attack seeing the two masked men running at her from up the stairs. Seeing the duffle bag of money on one of their shoulders, a look of alarm crossed her pretty brown face. She took a breath to yell.

"R-"

"Mmm!" Demetrius grunted sending a hay-maker to her face and knocking her out cold. "Shut up, bitch!"

There were still gunshots going on in the basement, letting Mario know that Rex was still alive and putting up a fight. He couldn't just leave him.

"Take the money and pull the car up."

"Bro—"

"I ain't leaving my fuckin' nigga, man!" Mario tossed Demetrius the car keys and the duffle bag. "If I ain't out in five minutes, drive off and drop off twenty Gs to my aunt."

Mario didn't give him a chance to answer before he took off toward the basement with his gun drawn. He took the concrete steps two at a time, trying to hurry up in case it wasn't too late.

"Nigga, you thought you could just come up into my bitch's spot and rob me like you was really about this life?"

Mario reached the bottom step of the basement just in time to see Rex scooting back, holding a gunshot wound at his waist. His gun was far away from him, like he'd dropped it when he got hit. The basement was cold and full of junk, boxes, and old furniture. Mario ducked behind one of the boxes so Ro wouldn't see his shadow.

"You're just a kid trying to play in a league with the big boys. Now, I'm about to split yo' shit open like I did your friend upstairs for trying to steal my money."

"Friends," Rex corrected.

"What did you say, little nigga?"

Ro knelt down and snatched Rex's mask from his face.

"I said, 'friends.' Plural, big nigga. You should tell yo' bitch to not be so chatty and niggas like me wouldn't have ran all up in her shit. I bet my niggas is around the block with your money right now. Ready to do it big."

He laughed and spat blood right into Ro's shocked face. Rex wasn't ready to die, but if this was his time, he wanted to go down fighting.

"Stupid nigga," Ro said, placing his gun to Rex's temple and putting pressure on the trigger. "I done seen your face. And when I go upstairs and take that nigga's mask off, I'ma see his too. Ain't gon' be nothing for my niggas to put two and two together on who robbed me. Yo' homies can thank you for getting them killed when I catch them."

"Nah," Mario said, standing up from where he was hiding. "*Real* niggas don't get caught."

He fired his gun four times when Ro whipped around and tried to aim his gun. It was no use. Mario caught him in the neck twice, his chest, and his stomach. When Ro dropped to the ground, he was staring blankly at the ceiling with no life left in him.

"Damn, nigga," Rex smiled dopily at his friend. "I thought you left me."

"Nah, nigga. Never that," Mario said, first grabbing Rex's gun and mask from the ground. After he tucked them away, he helped Rex up. "I would cross hella other niggas, but never *my* niggas. Come on, Demetrius is in the car waiting for us. We gotta hurry up before that nigga pulls off with the money."

Rex groaned as he limped up the stairs. They passed Lee's body on their way out the door and Rex's forehead wrinkled.

"He shot my dog, man," he said, shaking his head. "What I'ma tell his mom?"

"She knew he was a street nigga," Mario said bluntly. "This is the life we live; most likely will be how we die. At least he'll have an open casket."

Rex nodded his head and stepped over Tesha, who was still passed out in her living room right by her front door. Mario aimed his gun at her and squeezed the trigger twice, placing two bullets in her chest.

"No witnesses," he said heartlessly.

"Fuck!" Demetrius exclaimed when the two men stepped out of the house. He unlocked the car doors. "I was about to pull off on you niggas!"

"Pop the trunk!" Mario instructed after Rex was successfully placed in the car. "Come help me get the body."

He and Demetrius went back in the house to get Lee and put him in Mario's trunk.

"A'ight, now, let's go! Take me to my aunty. I can't go to the hospital after this shit. That's too hot. She can get the bullet out and patch me up. It's just a flesh wound. That nigga ain't have *no* aim on me."

"Hell, yes. Aunty Dez be working wonders," Demetrius nodded, knowing exactly who Rex was talking about. She was like a doctor to everyone in the hood.

They all drove in silence for a while. The hit had gone both good and bad. Lee wasn't someone that Mario had been close to. The only reason he was able to ride with them in the first place was because Rex plugged him. As fucked up as it sounded, his death didn't really move Mario too much. His mind was on the money and his future.

"Welp," Mario said, staring out the window as Demetrius drove, "at least I got the money for this date on Saturday."

"With Blake Rogers's daughter?"

"Yup. I'm getting all in that on Saturday. On God, nigga."

"How the fuck you pull that off? Word on the streets is that man don't let nobody near his precious baby girl."

"Nigga," Mario looked at Demetrius like he was crazy, "you know who I am? I get what I want when I want. Ain't nobody gon' stop me. Least of all Blake Rogers's bitch ass."

Demetrius reached his hand out and dapped his homie up one time.

"I feel you, my guy. She know who you are yet?"

"Nope," Mario said. "And I'm going to keep it that way until it's time. Now, hand me that bag so I can count this money. I guess we splitting it three ways instead of four."

Chapter 7

When Saturday came, Tiara kept her word to her parents. She didn't say a thing to them. She locked her bedroom door, and the only person she allowed to enter was Stephanie. She almost slipped up and told Stephanie about her plans for the night, but she didn't want to put her in the position to have to lie. Instead, she kept it to herself. Tiara passed her time by watching her favorite shows on TV and texting Brandy. Tiara hadn't even told her of the plans because she didn't want her to know just yet. Knowing Brandy, she would either try to talk her out of it, or she would just ask too many questions.

Cat tried to come to have a girls' talk with Tiara, but Tiara would not open the door for her. It was too late for all of that. She was trying to be a real mother too late. The seed of resentment was already planted too deeply in Tiara's heart. Instead of answering the knocks on her door, she opted to turn her TV up louder showing her mother blatant disrespect.

Fuck you, Tiara thought to herself.

The rest of the day time seemed to drag. She didn't know if it was because she was looking at the clock every five minutes or because time really was moving slow. It took a lifetime for the clock hands to finally read eleven o'clock. Tiara took a shower and got dressed. She put on a purple bra with the matching thong and slid a pair of black leggings up her legs and over her round ass. For her shirt, she opted for a black and red Chicago Bulls T-shirt. As for her hair, she put it all on the top of her head in a messy bun. After she sprayed herself with her Victoria's Secret perfume, she slid on a pair of socks and stuck her feet into her red UGG boots. She opened her bedroom door and peeked out of it while she tried to put her coat on silently. It was almost midnight now, so she was betting that her father wasn't home, and her mother was in bed sound asleep. She looked down the hall and kicked herself when she saw the door open. The lights were off, though, and the only light she could see was coming from the television, so maybe things would work in her favor.

Locking her door behind her, she checked her pocket to make sure she had the keys and her cell phone. Tiara crept along the wall like she was a nine-year-old sneaking downstairs to eat some cookies, and when she got to her parents' bedroom door, she peeked into the huge room. Just as she suspected, her father wasn't there, and her mother lay alone in the king-sized bed. That wasn't the best part, though. That night, her mother had decided to wear a mask that covered her eyes.

Tiara still didn't take any chances; she hurried past the doorway and toward the stairs without looking back at all. When she made it to the main floor she figured that going out the front door was not an option, so she continued walking as quietly as a mouse until she reached the basement. Once she was there, she went to the cold laundry room and shut that door behind her as well. Her eyes spotted the prize she was looking for, something that she could stand on. She found a crate in the corner and pulled it on the concrete floor to the window she was going to use to make her escape. She stood on top of the crate, on her tiptoes, and pushed the window open. As soon as she did, a huge gust of wind caught her by surprise. She had to inhale deeply before she could keep going. She quickly shut the window.

It was small, so Tiara knew it was going to be a tight fit, but she didn't care. All she could think about was seeing Mario. She looked out the window knowing that although none of her father's men were patrolling the area, there was still a camera somewhere.

"There!" she said to herself when she saw the rotating camera.

All she needed to do was time it just right. She counted the seconds in between its rotation and figured out that there was a seven-second window. The moment it started turning the other way, Tiara hoisted herself through the window. She had to wiggle her butt a little hard to get it through, but it worked. Once she was outside, she made a run for it. Checking her phone, she saw that it was just about to be midnight. There was a reason why she'd chosen that time. She knew that's when the night watch switched, and she also knew that they always left their post five minutes early before the next person came. Realizing that she only had a few minutes, she took out her phone and used the app on it to open the gate. She slid right on through and shut it back before it was even all the way opened.

She had made it! She walked straight down the neighborhood looking for Mario's car. Just when she thought that he must have forgotten about her, she saw the headlights of a car driving toward her. The Corvette pulled up next to her, and she heard the doors unlock. Without hesitation, she pulled the passenger door open and hopped in. Seeing Mario, she threw her arms around him and hugged him tightly.

"Wow," he said, admiring her. "You pulled that shit off."

Tiara grinned proudly like the Cheshire cat and let him go so that she could put her seat belt on.

"Where are we going?" she asked him.

"I got us a hotel suite not too far away from here," Mario said. "So we wouldn't have to be in the car the whole time."

"You think you're slick," Tiara's eyes lowered, and she bit her lip.

Mario laughed.

"What?" He lifted up the middle console and pulled out an already-rolled blunt and a lighter. "Stop talking shit and spark this."

"Gladly," Tiara said.

By the time they arrived at the Marriott that Mario had made reservations at, they were both so high they could barely feel their feet touching the ground. Since Mario had already checked in, all they had to do was get on the elevator and go up to their room.

"Here." Mario gave Tiara the room key so that she could open the door and enter first.

She did and was instantly filled with emotion. There were rose petals surrounding the king-sized bed and a bottle of Champagne chilling on ice on the nightstand beside it. On the bed, there were at least twenty miniature Snickers bars, her favorite chocolate, shaped into a heart.

"Oh, Mario," her hand shot to her mouth. "Nobody has ever done anything like this for me before!"

"Well, if you haven't ever gone on a regular date before I wouldn't doubt that," he joked, and she playfully pinched his arm. He took off his coat and helped her remove hers. Throwing them on one of the chairs he waved her to the bed. "Come on; have a glass of Champagne."

"You're only eighteen," Tiara said as she watched him pour her a glass. "How did you even get this stuff?"

"I have connections." Mario handed her the glass and poured his own. He lifted his glass in the air. "To us. May we always remain close, no matter what happens."

"To us," Tiara gushed and took the cup to the head.

She had smoked weed a lot and drank a little bit, but that was the first time that she had mixed the two. It was a pleasant feeling. Her body felt amazing when it was touched, and

Mario let his fingers trail up and down her arms ever so lightly. The two lay on the bed staring at the ceiling, talking and laughing.

"Have you ever just wanted to run away and never look back?" Tiara whispered, turning to face him.

She hadn't noticed how close they were until that very second. Her face was only inches away from his. She saw his lips twitch like he wanted to smile, but it showed as more of a grimace.

"Yeah," he said. "But this is my new life now . . . *You* are my new life."

"Promise?" Tiara's voice came out as more of a purr than a whisper, and Mario heard it.

He turned on his side so that he could face her. Nudging her nose with his, he placed his right hand on the back of her head.

"Promise," he said and pulled her lips to his.

The kiss was a deep, passionate one, and Tiara heard herself moaning into his mouth. She pressed her chest against him to let him know it was OK if he wanted to touch them. Her hands roamed freely on his muscular body, and she felt herself growing moist between her legs each time their tongues intertwined. Mario's hand slid under her T-shirt and massaged her breasts through her bra. Tiara's clit throbbed each time he pinched her nipple. Mario pulled away and looked at her. He traced her face with the finger-tip of his pointer finger and gazed into her eyes.

"Are you sure you want this?" he asked as he grabbed her hand and guided it toward the center of his pants.

Tiara was too far gone to tell him no. All she wanted was for him to make her feel good. So to answer his question, she sat up, took her shirt off, and unsnapped her bra. Mario licked his lips at the sight of her perky nipples.

"Lick them," Tiara instructed.

Mario sat up and palmed one of her titties, massaging it while he sucked the other. His tongue thumped her nipple, and he was pleased at the sounds coming from her mouth. He made her lie back down; then he went back and forth from each nipple until she started gyrating her hips, letting him know that something else needed some attention too. He planted kisses from her chest all the way to her navel. Her back arched in pleasure at the perfect timing. He was able to slide her leggings and panties off with the swiftness of a sex expert. When he saw her freshly shaven pussy and the juices flowing heavily from it, he wished he could dive right in it, but he knew that since she was a virgin, he would have to take his time. Plus, he wanted to taste it first. He removed his shirt, knowing that things were about to get more than a little messy.

"Tiara?" he breathed, kissing her thighs.

"Yes," she whispered into the air with her eyes shut.

"You are so beautiful." He let his lips brush against her clit, causing her to jump slightly. "Tiara?"

"Yessss."

"I love you," Mario said to her. "Do you love me?"

"Ye—"

Before she could fully answer his question, Mario took her clit inside of his mouth and sucked it relentlessly. Tiara's moan was so loud that she had to put a pillow over her head while Mario went to town between her legs. He ate her pussy so good that she pushed his head deeper and deeper into it. His tongue flicked on her clit until she felt it swell. Right when she released, Mario stuck his finger inside of her tight opening and finger fucked her while she was climaxing. Placing his mouth back over her clit, he sucked and pumped his finger at the same time, making her have back-to-back orgasms. His name was the only word that she seemed to know because she screamed it over and over. The feeling he was giving her was so good, and it beat the hell out of the vibrator she had at home.

Mario finally came up for air, and Tiara opened her eyes just a slit. She saw then that he must have removed his pants while he was giving her head because he positioned himself over her wearing nothing but a pair of Ralph Lauren boxers. Curious, she rubbed her hand against the bulge in his boxers and gave a tiny gasp. He was big, *really* big. Mario saw the fear in her eyes. He kissed her forehead. His dick was too hard, and she had already said yes. There was no turning back. But still, he wanted her to know it would be OK.

"I'll be gentle, OK, baby?" he said. Tiara nodded.

"Can I suck it first?" Tiara asked.

Those words were music to Mario's ears. The two switched positions, and Mario put his hands behind his head.

"Yo, don't bite me," Mario warned eyeing her. She was on the bed beside him positioned on her knees. "Arch your back some more. Yeah, like that. Put that phat ass in the air."

She gave him a devilish grin and did as she was told. She licked her lips and put them around the head of his eight-inch monster. She felt his hand on her ass and heard his moans. It urged her to continue. She tucked her teeth behind her lips and bobbed her head up and down. She used her free hand to jack him off at the same time as she was sucking. She was doing it so good that Mario's toes curled, and she could feel his nails digging into the meat on her butt.

"Ma, get on your back." Mario was unable to take it anymore. He pushed her head off of him and helped her lie comfortably on her back. She opened her legs wide, and he positioned the tip of his dick at her opening. "It's going to hurt at first, but after that, it's going to feel good. Bite me, scratch me, or scream loud as hell. Do whatever you need to, just don't tell me to stop, OK?"

"OK," Tiara said, gripping his back, preparing herself.

Mario pushed his dick a little farther into her tightness, and Tiara buried her head into his neck trying to stomach the pain. He pulled back and thrust again. That time, Tiara felt her hymen tear, and she moaned in pain.

"Shh, shhh," Mario rubbed her hair. "It's almost in, baby."

He thrust one last time, that time not so gentle, and pushed his shaft all the way in.

"Ahhh!" Tiara yelled out, scratching his back.

But he didn't stop. He held her steady, and at first, he fucked her slow, but when he felt her moans of pain turn into those of pleasure, he quickened his pace. She had the tightest and the wettest pussy he'd ever experienced in his life. He lifted up her legs and fucked her while rubbing on her clit. The way she had her face twisted up was turning him on even more.

"Mario! Mario!" she screamed when he turned her around and pounded into her from the back.

He was mesmerized by the way her yellow ass shook in the dim light of the hotel. He grabbed the Champagne glass and poured the liquid on her jiggly butt. The sight of the liquid streaming down made him go harder, and the sound of his dick going in and out of Tiara's wet box made him throw his head back and clench his eyes shut.

Tiara felt herself about to come again. She grabbed a fistful of her own hair in each hand. She didn't know how to throw her ass back, but all it took was two more pumps from Mario to make her squirt all on the bed below her.

"Oh my Gawwwd!" she screamed while her legs shook violently.

Mario too had reached his climax. He pulled himself out of Tiara's pussy and shot his nut all over her back. The two collapsed on top of the covers and held on to each other. Tiara knew that she could only sleep for a few hours before she had to get back home, but that was OK.

She'd had the best night ever. At that moment, a feeling of guilt came over her as she thought about the promise she'd made to her father so long ago.

"Welp," she said, "I can kiss that million good-bye."

"What's up?" Mario asked, but Tiara just snuggled deeper into her man's chest.

"Nothing," she said. "Wake me up in three hours, baby."

Chapter 8

Blake sat in the study of his office staring at the portrait he had drawn of his family when Tiara was only one year old. He sat in a chair fit for a king with a smiling Tiara sitting on his knee. Cat stood behind him with her hands on his shoulders. If only he could go back to those days and start over. He sighed. The weekend had come and gone, and Tiara still hadn't said a thing to them. He had planned to take her back to the basement and do some more target practice, but he knew he could just hang that up. She avoided them at all costs, and he wasn't even sure if she had eaten or not. He was beginning to think that maybe he should have just let her go on the date. He could have had his men follow them and keep an eye on her for him. Instead, he let his ego get the best of him, and he used his position of power against his daughter. He poured himself a shot of vodka. His cell phone vibrated. He answered it before he took the drink to the head.

"Hello?"

"I'm about to kill your daughter," a gruff voice said on the other end.

"Who the fuck is this?" Blake demanded.

"You have much worse problems on your hands than knowing who I am," the voice said. "Right now, your daughter is walking to her lunch table in the cafeteria holding her tray tightly. She's smiling right now because she doesn't have a clue that she's about to die."

"If you touch her I'll—"

"You'll *what?* Star sixty-nine me? I'm about to show you what it feels like to lose a loved one!"

Click.

Blake didn't know if it was a prank call or what, but either way, he moved as fast as he possibly could to round up his men and send them to his daughter's school before it was too late.

"You didn't talk to them at all?" Brandy was saying to Tiara after they set their trays on the lunch table.

"Nope," Tiara told her. "He didn't even have a real reason why I couldn't go. He was just trying to be controlling. I swear, as soon as I can, I'm out of that house!"

"You don't seem too angry, though," Brandy said, eyeballing her friend. "You've actually been smiling all day. What happened that you aren't telling me about?"

Tiara's grin was enough, and she didn't even have to say a thing for Brandy to get it.

"Oh my goodness!" Brandy exclaimed and pushed her tray of food out of her way. She had suddenly lost her appetite. "Bitch . . . Did you guys fuck?"

Tiara nodded her head, still smiling like a maniac. Brandy stood up and went to the other side of the table to sit next to Tiara. She grabbed Tiara's hands and looked into her eyes.

"How the fuck did you pull that off?"

"You know that small window in the basement at my house? I snuck out of it."

"You mean to tell me you got that ass through that small-ass window?"

"Yes, girl! The struggle was too real!" They both laughed.

"Oh my God. I can't believe you had the guts to sneak out of your house like that." Her friend was in disbelief. "How did you even get past all of the security cameras and shit? You must've done some 007 shit for real, bitch!" The girls high-fived each other and laughed again.

"Seriously, though, that window is the only blind spot to the security guards. The camera will still pick it up, but I waited for it to rotate the other way. Mario was waiting down the street, and when I made it through the gate, we just spent the rest of the night together. It was so amazing."

"Did it hurt?"

"Hell, yes, it hurt! But it was like a good pain, I guess. He was so sweet. He held me the whole time."

"Did you suck his dick?"

"He's my nigga. Why wouldn't I suck his dick?"

Brandy squealed and clapped her hands together.

"That's why you're my bitch!" The two girls talked about Tiara losing her virginity for the rest of their lunch hour. Brandy told her that she was proud that she'd finally taken a stand for herself and done something exciting for the first time in her young life. The girls were finished with their food and were clearing out their table getting ready to put their trays in the lunch bins.

"Who are they?" She looked at the lunch ladies and the new lunch guys helping them take the food back into the kitchen. "I've never seen those guys before, have you?"

Brandy stood and looked up just as she was about to take her trash to the trash can. Since she'd started attending Burton, the lunch workers had been the same. Tiara stood up with her tray too and stared at the guys Brandy was talking about. There were four of them, and Tiara made a weird face.

"Why are there four of them? I didn't know the lunch ladies needed that much help."

The question hadn't even been out of her mouth for a full second when the men noticed Tiara was staring at them. There were two black men, one white man, and one Hispanic. One of the black guys smiled sinisterly at Tiara before shouting, "Now!"

All four men then threw their lunch attire over their heads, revealing black suits and automatic weapons. Tiara saw it before it happened, but it was too late. She tried to grab Brandy when she took cover under their table in the cafeteria, but the bullets from the shooter ripped into Brandy's body, making her twitch violently.

"Brandy! Brandy!" Tiara screamed repeatedly, holding on to her friend's body when it dropped to the ground.

Brandy tried to say something, but it came out sounding like a gurgle. Blood poured from her mouth, and Tiara tried to apply pressure to her wounds. Chaos was all around her, and the screaming of her fellow classmates were coming from every direction. Tiara stared down at her friend, and all the commotion seemed to fade in the background. They were loud, but Tiara couldn't hear them. The only thing she was focused on was her best friend lying in her arms choking on her own blood. Brandy feverishly reached for Tiara's hand and squeezed it tightly.

"I love you, Brandy, You are my very best friend," Tiara whispered, letting her tears fall on Brandy's face.

Brandy gave her what was supposed to be a smile. "I-I love y-you too, T. P-please don't f-forget me, OK?"

"I promise," Tiara sobbed. "I won't. Never ever."

Before Tiara could say anything else, she felt Brandy's grip on her hand slacken and watched her opened eyes go dim. Tiara let go of Brandy's hand and shut her eyes to make it look as though she was just sleeping. Placing Brandy's head to her chest, she buried her head in Brandy's hair and sobbed. She didn't care if a bullet caught her right then and there. The one person in the world who understood her all the way was gone. The pain she felt was unlike anything she had ever experienced. It was like a piece of her died along with her friend. She could feel the void already. She shook and sobbed into Brandy's hair, silently praying for her to please come back. She didn't plan on ever letting her go until she felt a hand grip her shoulder tightly.

"Tiara, we have to go!"

Tiara looked up to see Mario standing over her. When she tried to pull away from him, he jerked her arm harder. "It's too late for Brandy, but we have to get out of here now. They came for you!"

They came for you! His words echoed in her head.

The bullets that were made for her had slaughtered Brandy instead. Tiara kissed her forehead.

"I'm so sorry, Brandy," she whispered. "I'm so sorry."

"Come on, Tiara! Your dad's men are in here, but I don't know how much longer they can hold them off!"

Tiara finally listened to reason and laid Brandy's body down gently. "I'll come back for you," Tiara promised and struggled to her feet.

The two of them ran as quickly as they could away from the gunfire. Tiara almost couldn't stomach the sight of all the bodies of students she kept stumbling across. Some were still alive while others were dead in pools of blood.

"Ahh!" Mario yelled as a bullet grazed his arm.

"Mario!" Tiara cried out.

"I'm OK." Mario winced at the wound. "It just grazed me. Keep going. My car is in the back of the building."

They made it out of the building without any other occurrences and ran all the way to Mario's red Corvette, hand in hand. He put the key in the ignition and floored the gas pedal all the way to Tiara's house. Right before they got to the gate, Tiara asked Mario to pull over. She opened the passenger-side door and leaped out. Everything that was in her stomach came out instantly, and she tried to catch her breath.

"Hey, hey," Mario rubbed her back.

He felt her long hair under his slender fingers as his hand went back and forth between her shoulder blades. He felt her heart thumping fast while she continued to take deep breaths. It wasn't until then that he noticed that she was covered in blood, and her face was completely pale.

"Come on," Mario said. "Let's get you home. Your parents are probably really worried about you."

Tiara nodded and shut her door. Mario drove up to the gate and saw an armed man standing there. He walked up to the driver's-side window, and Mario rolled it down.

"Can you please tell Mr. Rogers that I have his daughter Tiara with me?"

The guard's face changed, and he looked over into the passenger's side. When he saw that it, in fact, was Tiara, he opened the gate up and waved them through. At the same time, he radioed to the house that Tiara was home. Tiara pointed out her house to Mario. He helped her out of the car and up the steps that led to the front door. Tiara pushed it open, and as soon as she stepped into the house, she was bombarded with a swarm of people around her.

"Oh my God, she's been shot!" Stephanie shrieked when she saw Tiara covered in blood.

"No, Stephanie, it's not my blood!" Tiara yelled out. "I'm okay; it's not mine!"

"Oh, thank God! I was so worried!" Stephanie was the first person to embrace her. She pulled away and examined her with wide eyes. "Why— how are you covered in blood?"

"I-it's not mine," Tiara was able to get out. She wanted to say more, but she didn't have the strength. She felt emotionally exhausted.

Cat came forward and pulled Tiara away from Stephanie to hug her daughter.

"I'm glad you're OK, baby," she said into Tiara's ear as she embraced her daughter. "We got the call that somebody was shooting at the school, and we thought the worst. Your father is on his way back here now."

Tiara pulled away and just nodded her head. She was numb all over. All she wanted to do was go to her room and sleep. Maybe when she woke up it would have all just been one horrible nightmare. Everyone around her began bombarding her with a million and one questions. The only voice she heard was Stephanie's.

"If that isn't your blood, Tiara, whose is it?"

Tiara's eyes welled with tears all over again, and her bottom lip trembled. She opened her mouth to speak, but she couldn't bring herself to say a word. The image of Brandy lying dead in the school's cafeteria entered her head, and it was too much for her to bear in one day.

"I think she's been through enough for one day," Mario finally spoke up from behind them all.

All eyes turned to where the voice had come from.

"Who are you?" Cat asked. "What is he doing here?"

"My name is—"

"Tiara!" Blake Rogers's voice boomed throughout the house when he pushed the door open and saw his daughter standing there.

He left his security guards outside of the house and rushed to swoop her up off of the ground. He held her tightly to him like she was just a baby and kissed her face. When he put her back down, he studied her from top to bottom.

"You have blood all over you," he observed. "Are you OK?"

"It's not my blood," Tiara said, struggling with her speech. "It's . . . It's Brandy's! She's dead!"

She was finally able to say it, and Stephanie gasped. She had to take a seat. Stephanie then knew why Tiara's face was so pale; her best friend had been murdered right before her eyes. From the looks of it, Tiara must have held her until the end.

"No!" she exclaimed. "Oh, Lord, not Brandy."

"Daddy," Tiara looked up into Blake's eyes, "is it true that those men came looking for me today? Is it true that they wanted to kill me?"

Instead of answering, Blake looked to Cat for help. She came and stood by his side. Gripping his hand, she tried to talk to Tiara.

"Honey—"

"They meant to kill me!" Tiara screamed. "They killed Brandy instead! But they were trying to kill me!"

Tiara was hysterical by then. Her sobs were uncontrollable, and she looked at both of her parents with deep anger in her eyes.

"Tiara—" her mother tried again. That time she reached for Tiara, but Tiara pushed her hand away.

"Fuck you!" she screamed. "This is all *his* fault!" She pointed a finger at her father. "My best friend is dead! She's dead, and she's not coming back!" Tiara had to take a breath. She backed away until she got to the stairs that would take her up to her room. Her face was completely twisted, and she cried like a five-year-old child. She turned and looked around the room. "I hate all of you! I don't want to live like this anymore! I have lost the only person in this world that ever truly gave a fuck about me, and you all are just standing there nonchalant as hell like *I'm* the only one with blood on my body! Her blood is on everybody, not just me!"

With that, she turned and ran up the stairs, leaving all of them to stand there in an awkward silence. Stephanie nodded her respects to Mario for bringing her home safely and ran up the stairs after her. Blake wiped his face with his hand and tried to make sense of what had just happened.

***

By the time that he and his men had arrived at the scene, the shooters were already dead. He couldn't understand why they had even gone to the trouble of invading the school in the first place. The first person that came to his mind was Rodriguez, but regardless of the fact that Blake had pretty much taken over his operation by force, he still had a major hand in all of the dealings. He was making more money in the heroin game being partnered up with Blake than he ever had running things solo. Until he figured out exactly what was going on and who called the hit, he would need his security to be doubled. He was deeply saddened by Brandy's death; he knew how close she and Tiara had been. She was the first real friend Tiara ever had that didn't use her for the perks of having a truly rich friend. However, he would have been lying if he said he wasn't glad it was her and not Tiara. Mentally, he made a note to write Brandy's family a check to cover the entire funeral, and more.

Blake finally noticed the tall boy standing in the room with them. He looked a mess, and he had blood dripping down his arm. Blake could tell the boy was trying to decide whether he should leave or go upstairs after Tiara. From the concerned look in his eyes, he guessed that this was the boy that his daughter had begged to go on a date with.

"Mario, right?" Blake said, catching the boy off guard.

"Yes, sir, Mr. Rogers. Sir," Mario stammered.

"Are you all right?" he said as he gestured toward Mario's bloodstained arm.

"I'm all right, sir. A bullet grazed my arm, that's all. It's nothing I can't handle."

"I was told that you were the one who rescued my daughter and brought her home," Blake said, walking to Mario and standing directly in front of him. "Is that true?"

"Yes."

Blake sized Mario up, and then finally nodded his head. He held out his hand for Mario to shake it.

"Thank you," Blake said. "I apologize that you had to witness that. Please have one of my guys take a look at the wound on your arm."

"No need to thank me, sir. It was no problem at all," Mario said, shaking Blake's hand. "I'm just glad she's OK. And my arm will be fine. I was one of the lucky ones. If it's all right with you, I would like to check on Tiara before I leave."

Blake contemplated the boy's words. He knew that the right thing to do was allow him to go upstairs and console his daughter, especially since his face was probably one of the only ones she could stomach. Blake waved his hand to the stairs.

"I might have been wrong about you," Blake said, remembering how hard he'd been on his daughter's crush. "Go on. When you come back down, my security will let you out. I have some business to attend to, and I'm sure my wife will be in bed."

"Thank you, sir," Mario said and hurried past him.

Halfway up the stairs, Blake Rogers surprised him again. "And Mario?" he said.

"Yes, sir?"

"Come over on Sunday. I would be honored if you joined us for dinner."

Mario was shocked, but instead of showing it on his face, he flashed Blake the best smile he could muster given the grimness of the situation.

"I would love to, sir. Thank you."

Chapter 9

Tiara was allowed to miss school the rest of the week. She couldn't find the strength to get up and go back into that place. All she had been thinking about was Brandy. Her family laid her to rest only two days after, and the funeral was hard to attend. She sat in the front along with the rest of Brandy's family and clung to Brandy's mother like her life depended on it. She was able to say her final good-byes to her best friend, and although she was sure Brandy was at peace, she wasn't. There was an ache in her heart because she felt that Brandy's murder was completely her fault. If Brandy wouldn't have been friends with Tiara in the first place, then she wouldn't have been sitting at that lunch table, and she would still be alive. She thought of all the times they shared and looked through all the selfies they'd taken in her phone. Spring was literally around the corner, and she couldn't believe she would be bringing in her eighteenth birthday without her best friend.

Tiara cried every day after the funeral and stayed locked in her room. She didn't eat; she just lay there feeling sick. The only thing that provided her solace was the fact that her father had invited Mario over for dinner on Sunday. She knew he'd only done that because he felt guilty for further ruining her life. But she would take it. Mario was the only other person that she felt she had left in the world. She had distanced herself from everyone, including Stephanie. The only person who heard her voice was her boyfriend. When Sunday night finally came, she showered and actually combed her hair. She got dressed and wore a pretty cream-colored dress and a pair of brown flats. Her hair flowed around her shoulders. She finally opened her bedroom door to show her face to the rest of the house. She smelled the amazing scent of her mother and the cooks making all of their favorite foods, and she heard her father and his friends in the living room watching some sports game. She told Mario to be there at eight. At seven-fifty the doorbell rang.

She beat the housekeeper to the door and flung it open. Sure enough, on the other end of the door was her boo holding a bouquet of roses. He smiled at her when he saw her.

"Wow, you look amazing, ma," he said, handing her the roses.

"Thank you, you do too," Tiara said, taking in the black designer suit that he chose to wear that night.

The two snuck a quick kiss, and she led him into the foyer of the house.

"Just the person I wanted to see!" Blake said, coming from up behind the two teenagers. "Come sit down. The food is ready."

He took them into the dining room where the long table was already almost filled to capacity with food and people surrounding it. Blake sat at the head of the table with Tiara to his left and Cat to his right. Mario took a seat next to Tiara and ignored the curious stares he was receiving from everyone at the table. He was there for one reason and one reason only, and that reason was not to mingle with the likes of them. Tiara grabbed his hand under the table, and he smiled at her. Like always, Blake requested for everyone to bow their heads as he said the prayer before anyone dug into the food.

"So, Mario, my daughter tells me that you are in the same grade as her at school," Cat said after everyone had loaded up their plates.

"Yes, I am, Mrs. Rogers," he answered her as he swallowed a forkful of rice.

"What are your plans after graduation?"

"I hope to go to a college on the West Coast so I can study to become an architect," he answered with a smile.

Cat nodded, seemingly pleased with his response. Everyone else seemed engaged in their own conversations, but Blake and Cat were focused more on Mario. Blake didn't know what it was, but there was something about Mario that he recognized from somewhere. However, he was certain that he'd never seen the youngster before.

"Do you have any family here in Dallas?" Blake asked, taking a couple of bites of his food.

"I live with my aunt," Mario told him. And before Blake could ask he said, "My dad died when I was a little kid, and my mom never really got over his death. She just couldn't handle the pain of him being gone, and she turned to drugs. Her body is still alive, but the drugs practically killed her. I don't know where she is."

"I'm so sorry," Cat said, her voice dripping with sympathy. "Well, I'm glad your aunt took you in. That's an absolute blessing. Things could have been much worse, and you could have been lost in the system."

"Tell me about it," Mario said. "I'm too fine for foster care!"

Even Blake laughed at that, and Tiara felt herself becoming less tense. The dinner went without a hitch, and everyone was getting along just fine. Tiara even found herself smiling and being nice to her mother. When dinner was over, all of their guests left except for Mario. Blake whisked him off to show him around the house, leaving the two women and the staff behind to clean off the table and wash the dishes.

"He seems nice," Cat said to her daughter. "You like him a lot, huh?"

"Yeah, I do," Tiara said, drying the dishes that were in the dish drainer. "He's an amazing person."

"I remember when I first met your father," Cat said dreamily. "I recall the feeling he gave me, and the first time we—"

"Mommy!" Tiara exclaimed and put her wet hands to her ears.

Cat giggled like a schoolgirl. "Well, I'm just saying, that man is something else. We go through it, but at the end of the day, I know he'll always make sure I'm all right," she said. Suddenly, she sighed. "Tiara, I know that we haven't had the best relationship since you've come into your teenage years. And now with Brandy gone and you about to leave home soon, I would like to fix that. I don't want to lose you."

Tiara pondered over her words for a few moments and was tempted to tell her to go shove them up her ass. But she knew that being bitter wouldn't help the situation any, either, so instead of being mean, she nodded her head.

"OK, Mommy, I won't say that it will be an overnight thing. But I will try if you will try."

Cat cocked her head and touched her daughter's cheek. She sometimes didn't think she had anything to do with her daughter's being there. The only thing Tiara got from Cat was her physique and her high cheekbones; other than that, she was her father's child completely. They made small talk and laughed together for a few more minutes before Tiara took her leave to find her father and her boyfriend.

"I'll be right back, Mommy," she said and handed her mother the towel she had been using to dry the dishes.

Blake had led Mario upstairs to his study and shut the double doors behind them. He then lit a Cuban cigar and handed it to Mario, who took it and puffed a little too hard. He broke into a coughing fit, and Blake patted his back, finding humor in Mario's struggle.

"You need more practice," Blake said, taking the cigar back from him.

"It looks that way, huh?" Mario said and wiped the water from his eyes. "I think I'll give myself a few more years before I try that again."

Blake went and sat behind his desk. He blew on his cigar and motioned for Mario to have a seat across from him. When Mario sat down, the two men looked at each other.

"What are your intentions with my daughter, Mario?" Blake asked the question he didn't want to ask during dinner when Tiara was around. He knew she would have thrown a fit and it would've ruined the evening. He was happy to see his daughter smiling and laughing tonight. Her happiness meant everything to him.

"Happiness," Mario answered as if he had read Blake's mind.

"What about it?" Blake asked.

"Gaining happiness and giving happiness are my intentions." Mario explained, "I've had a bit of a rough life, and things haven't been easy. I've been failed by a lot of people, and I've come to realize that if you want your life to get better, then you have to do it yourself. All I want is to make a way out for myself and be able to provide happiness, comfort, and stability to the ones I love."

"Are you saying you love my daughter?" Blake stared into the young man's eyes. He was a little taken aback by Mario's boldness.

"Yes, sir, I do," Mario answered confidently.

"I see," Blake responded. He took another drag of his cigar without saying anything. He was genuinely impressed with what Mario was saying to him. He was expecting a young, naïve little schoolboy to show up for dinner. He was surprised to learn that his daughter had chosen a seemingly smart and strong young man like Mario to stand by her side.

"Well, I like what I'm hearing, son." Blake smiled at Mario. "I owe you a great debt for what you did back at the school that day. You showed a lot of courage, and you saved my daughter's life. I can never repay you for that." Mario stayed quiet as he saw Blake take another pull from his cigar.

"You have my blessing to date my daughter." Blake was about to stand up and shake Mario's hand, but Mario's next words stopped him in his tracks.

"Oh, I don't need your motherfucking blessing."

"Excuse me?" Blake asked calmly.

"It's fucked up," Mario said, shaking his head.

"What do you mean by that, son?"

"That you have such an amazing daughter, but her shit is all fucked up because of you." Mario began to laugh evilly. His whole demeanor seemed to change instantly. "I'ma just stop now with the charades, my nigga. Tiara is cool, and I almost feel bad for using her to get what I really wanted. But truth be told, I honestly don't give a *fuck* about her happiness. All I care about is mine. I'm not here for her. I came for me. But above that, I came here for *you*."

"I'm sorry, what was that last thing you said?" Blake asked, not sure if he'd heard him correctly.

"Exactly what I said. I came for you," Mario repeated. "Your biggest mistake tonight was letting me enter your home without having your security check me," he said as he pulled a pistol from his waist. "Put your gun on the table and we can talk some more."

Mario pointed his weapon at Blake's head, but Blake sat unmoving, staring into Mario's hateful eyes.

"I am in my home," Blake said evenly. "I am unarmed."

Mario kept his gun aimed at Blake's head and went over to the other side of the desk to check to see if he was being lied to. When he was sure that Blake really did not have any weapon, he put his gun to the back of Blake's head and made them switch seats.

"How does it feel?" Mario asked sitting in the king's chair. "To know you've been tricked. To know that your daughter has been tricked. You let me walk right into your home. It was almost too easy."

"Why don't you tell me who you are?" Blake said, his voice still even. "Who you *really* are."

The gun pointed at his head did not intimidate him; however, it bothered him that he had no clue who the person sitting in front of him was.

Who has my daughter allowed in my house? he asked himself.

"Look at me," Mario demanded. "Tell me who *you* see."

Blake couldn't say. Mario's face had looked familiar from the first day he saw him, but he was sure he had never seen the boy until the day of the shooting.

"You don't know, do you? I guess with all the bodies you must have under your belt, it's hard to remember one from years ago, huh?" Mario shook his head.

"You just said that you were done with the charades," Blake said in a bored tone. "But it seems to me that you're still playing them. I don't do guessing games."

"Diablo!" Mario screamed in Blake's face. "You killed my fucking uncle!"

Blake's mouth opened slightly, but he quickly shut it. It all made sense to him. Mario looked so much like Diablo he could have smacked himself for not making the connection. It had been so long since he had seen Diablo's face. He had heard of the past coming back to hurt him, and Blake was a sure believer in Karma; he just didn't know it would catch up to him so soon. Especially since he had just wrapped up such a large business deal.

"Look, son, I don't expect you to understand," Blake said. "You were just a boy back when it happened. I don't know what you've been told about it growing up, but I can assure you, your uncle was robbing me."

"Because you weren't paying him enough money!" Mario screamed.

It was all coming out. Blake was right; Mario was a little boy when someone came knocking on his aunt's door to tell her that her husband was dead and that they had to immediately evacuate the house because they could no longer live in it. From that night on, Mario had been forced to grow up and do things that were beyond his years. He watched his aunt struggle working odd jobs just to put food on the table and keep a roof over their heads. Little Mario started cutting grass and raking leaves to make money to help out, but it just wasn't cutting it. Eventually, he turned to doing small robberies. He would break into a few cars and take whatever he could find. From there, he moved on to breaking into houses. One night he was almost caught when the man whose house he was robbing started shooting at him. He was able to fight the man to the ground and take his gun. When he felt that cold steel metal in his hand, he felt whole. He developed a passion for guns and trained himself how to use them. Before he knew it, he had made a reputation for being quick with his hands and swift with his guns and began doing work for hire.

He had always wondered about what happened to his uncle, and after he finally learned the truth, he had been on a mission to avenge his death. When he heard that a man by the name of Tommy Rodriguez had a price on Blake's head, he jumped at the opportunity. He felt it was a win-win for him; he would get revenge on his uncle's killer and get paid for doing it.

For Rodriguez, hiring this young kid was the perfect setup. He had learned that Blake was getting ready to come in on his territory and seize control of the majority of his business, and that is something Rodriguez could not allow. He had come seeking help from Diablo's only living uncle, Carlos, to exact revenge, but he learned that Carlos had retired and left the life of being an assassin behind him. He was heading out when Mario approached him and offered to do the job. Rodriguez thought that Mario was young, bloodthirsty, but he saw the passion in his eyes, so he decided to give him a shot. Rodriguez came up with the plan of having Mario get to Blake through his daughter Tiara. He paid Mario's school tuition, and he and Mario planned everything out. Mario came in to that school determined to win Tiara over; otherwise, he would never be able to get anywhere near Blake.

Mario was enrolled into the same school as Tiara Rogers, but he never bet on her being as beautiful and down-to-earth as she was. He never bet on truly falling for her, but his mission was just more important. What had happened in the cafeteria was his doing as well. Rodriguez sent his own soldiers disguised as lunch helpers to start a massacre in the middle of her lunch period. It all was a ploy to make Mario look like a hero. Even the graze on his arm was staged. He never meant for Tiara's best friend to get killed, but there are casualties in all wars. She was already so broken, and it pained him to hurt her even more, but after he was done there, he would move on and never look back. Tiara would just be a memory, and a hefty bank account would be his new girlfriend.

"Diablo was trying to take care of his family!" Mario yelled again. "After you killed him, I had to sit and watch my aunt struggle every day trying to survive just because you couldn't keep your end of the bargain. You'd been skimping Diablo on his money for years! *Years!* Anything he took from you was rightfully owed, you slimy bitch-ass nigga!"

Mario applied pressure to the trigger, but he wasn't able to get a shot off because Blake reached over and hit the gun out of his hand. Blake caught him with a right hook so hard that Mario felt like the room was experiencing an earthquake. But he recuperated fast and came back at Blake with a combination of power punches to his gut. Where Blake excelled in power, Mario had speed. For every one powerful blow that Blake landed, Mario landed three. Unknown to Blake, Mario had a knife in his belt as well. Blake went to slam Mario to the ground, but while he held him in mid-air, Mario was able to retrieve the knife and shoved it straight into Blake's chest.

"Ahh!" Blake cried out in pain and dropped Mario to the ground.

He staggered back and yanked the knife from his chest. He put his massive hand over the wound, but it was no help. Blood gushed through his fingers and dripped on his clean carpet, staining it. Blake's breathing was short, and he fell down to the ground with his back against his desk. He tried to reach for the phone in his pocket. All he had to do was hit one button for his security to sweep the building clean and save him. However, a kick to his temple stopped any feeble attempt at a rescue.

"The fuck you think you're doing?" Mario had gotten back to his feet and was now punching and kicking Blake all over his body.

Blake's face had started to swell already from all of the hits Mario had landed on it. Mario had the gun once again in his hand and pointed it at Blake. He almost laughed at how easy it all had been. The sight of Blake's bloody and defeated body made Mario feel powerful.

"Any last words?" Mario panted aiming the gun at a spot between Blake's eyes.

Blake sat there awaiting death, ready for it. His only regret was that he wasn't going to be able to see his daughter one last time and tell her that he loved her and that none of this was her fault. In that moment, he understood what Tiara meant when she said she had never asked for this life. Although he was proud of the lavish and comfortable life he had been able to provide for her, he had also brought her into a dark and dangerous world that she had no business being in. With him gone, he worried about who was going to be able to protect her.

"T-tell Tiara that it wasn't her fault," Blake said to Mario. "Don't let her live with this grief on her soul. T-tell her I always loved her."

Mario nodded his head. "Sure, old man. By the way, Rodriguez sends his love."

Bang!

Chapter 10

Blood. All Tiara saw was the blood. The smile that was once plastered on her face vanished the moment she slid the doors to her father's study open. All the laughter in her chest washed away, only to be replaced with a seething pain with the sight she saw. There, the notorious Blake Rogers lay on his back with his eyes still wide open and a neat red dot between them. Tiara caught herself on the door handle and slapped her hand to her mouth to stifle whatever sound dared to escape her lips. Her breathing was short and quick as her eyes darted around the room looking for the intruder. The only thing she saw was an open window and the particles from the back of her father's head plastered on everything from the curtains, to the windows, to the wall. There was even a little bit of red splatter on the ceiling.

"Dad—" Tiara croaked finally, her voice was barely audible. "Daddy!"

Her whole body shook violently, and she dropped to the ground. Her tongue tasted salty, and she realized that tears were sliding down her face and landing inside her quivering mouth. She crawled from the entrance of the study to her father's lifeless body. As she crawled, the knees of her dress got stained with blood. When she got to his body, she shook him, hoping that he would wake up. But his eyes held the same dull look that Brandy's had when she held her in the cafeteria. He was gone. Tiara finally caught her breath and let out a bloodcurdling scream that could be heard throughout the whole house.

Within seconds, Cat and Stephanie entered the study.

"We heard a commo—" Cat started, but when she saw the scene before her she almost had a heart attack. "Oh God, no."

She dropped down to the ground and crawled just as Tiara had toward Blake's body.

"Baby," she shook him. "Blake! No no no. You promised you wouldn't leave me. Please, baby, wake up!"

She then started screaming too. Stephanie stared in horror but was able to radio to the security downstairs to check the perimeters of their property for the culprit. She couldn't believe it. Blake Rogers was dead. Suddenly she thought of something. She had seen Blake and Mario enter Blake's study alone after dinner. Maybe he saw something.

"Tiara," Stephanie said, snapping her out of her deep trance. "Tiara, where is Mario?"

Tiara wasn't in a position to answer any questions, but the security guard who had just entered the room was able to give them an answer.

"He just left not even five minutes ago," the guard said. "He looked a bit dinged up, like he got into a fight."

"*He did this!*" Cat screamed while she sobbed. "He killed my husband! Oh my God, he killed my husband! Blake! Blake!"

The remainder of the night was a blur. When the paramedics arrived, Blake Rogers was pronounced dead at the scene. Cat threw her body on the stretcher not wanting them to take her husband away. Vincent arrived not too long after and couldn't believe his eyes. His cousin was dead. At first, he thought it was a joke, not believing anybody could take out an ox like Blake, but when he saw it for himself, there was no denying it. The first thing he did was speak to the police officers and federal agents who were glad to have a reason to come snooping around Blake's residence. Tiara and Cat went with them to fill out a report, and Vincent sent the rest of them on their way after all of the pictures of the murder scene were taken.

Once the coast was clear, he went to the recording console that Blake kept in the house. In there were at least twenty different TV screens of the video surveillance Blake had on his house and his neighborhood. He played back the video of what had happened in Blake's study that night and witnessed Tiara's boyfriend killing him. He also heard everything he said to Blake. Right when Mario was about to pull the trigger and he said that Rodriguez had sent him, Vincent turned off the recording. He bet that Rodriguez thought that nobody would find out that Blake was killed under his order. Vincent also bet that Blake knew that Rodriguez might turn foul and had a spy in Rodriguez's most trusted counsel ready to pull the trigger on call. He took out his phone and dialed a number.

"Pull the plug and bleed that whole motherfucking thing dry. The Eagle is down. Plans have changed."

Chapter 11

Attending the funeral of her father was not something Tiara planned on doing so soon. She was lost. Her best friend was already six feet under, and now her father would be too. Tiara walked up the pews with her mother just a few steps ahead of her. She watched as her mother walked with her head held high like the queen that she was. Despite the relationship that they had, Tiara saw her mother in a different light after seeing how she was handling the situation. Whenever she thought about her mom, she never considered her strong or brave, but seeing her mother walk down the aisle with such confidence and finesse really showed Tiara that when it came to her mom, there was more than meets the eye. Tiara did her best to follow in her mother's footsteps and looked straight-ahead at the pulpit before her. She did her best to avoid the stares of those around them. She heard somebody whisper the word "devil" when she walked by, and Tiara had to pretend she heard nothing. It hurt her heart to know that she was blamed by the whole community for her father's death. Even her mother showed that she had some resentment toward her. She was glad that the veil from her hat covered the tears sliding down her face.

Blake had a glorious home going. Vincent made sure he sat beside Tiara. He had heard Blake's final request. Although everyone was making her feel like she wasn't worth two nickels rubbed together, he wanted her to know that she was the last thought on her father's mind before he died. He held her hand the whole service and allowed her to ride with him to the grave site. Tiara kept her head down, and she stayed back while everyone else threw their roses on the casket when it was lowered into the earth. When everyone left, Tiara walked slowly to the casket. She kissed her white rose and sent a silent prayer to her father. She hoped that wherever his soul rested that he was at peace, and she apologized for bringing evil into his home. With one last good-bye, she threw her rose on the casket that her father's body was in.

"I love you, Dad," she whispered into the wind chill. "Always."

Vincent came behind her and threw his rose on the casket as well. He put his arm around her and hugged her.

"Come on, Princess, let me get you home," he said.

"What home?" Tiara asked, shrugging her shoulders. "My mother hates me."

"She doesn't hate you."

"She does," Tiara said, her voice shaky. "She can't stand to even look at me, and when she does, I can see the hatred in her eyes."

Vincent didn't know what to say because knowing the type of attitude Cat had, Tiara was probably telling the truth. Instead of trying to console Tiara, she most likely was shunning her like she'd done even when Blake was still alive. Vincent had always felt a closeness with Tiara ever since she'd saved his life. He knew that her heart was kind and this was something she wouldn't have wished on anyone. He knew that the way she thought and acted was a result of her upbringing, but Cat would never take responsibility for that.

"Come on," Vincent urged. "We will come and visit his burial site often. I promise we will still have our special moments with him."

Tiara followed him back to his Mercedes-Benz and got in the passenger seat. Before they pulled away, Tiara asked her cousin a question.

"Do you think Daddy hates me?"

"Never, my love," Vincent told her. "Blake loved you with all that he had. If anything, he is hoping from his grave that *you* don't hate *him*. I am now in charge of all of your father's business, and the person who ordered the hit won't even have a funeral. I want you to know that regardless of whatever happens, you will be set for life. I'm leaving for New York. With your father gone, there is nothing left for me here. But if you ever need me for anything, just call me. I will never change my number."

With that, he pulled away from the grave site and let the others pay their respects. He nodded his head at the hired hands he had guarding his cousin's grave site making sure that nobody would come and be disrespectful. He drove Tiara back home and kissed her on her forehead.

"I love you, Princess," Vincent said.

"I love you too, Cousin Vincent," Tiara said, trying to give him a smile.

It was a weak one, but he was happy that she was even able to muster that one up. She waved her final farewell to Vincent Rogers and walked in the house. When she entered the house, there were many people there. All Tiara saw was black, and she just wanted to make it to her bedroom. When she walked past a few people, they stopped their conversations mid-sentence. She knew that they were most likely talking about her. She looked around in search of her mother. When she finally saw her across the room, she saw a crowd of people surrounding her. From where she stood, she could hear that people were offering words of encouragement and their condolences.

When Cat's eyes fell on Tiara, they became daggers, and her nose flared in disgust. Tiara felt like the scum of the earth. To make matters worse, she had no one to turn to. Her best friend was dead, and her boyfriend had turned out to be her ultimate enemy.

"Get her out of here! Why is she just standing there?" Tiara heard her mother say as Cat pointed in her daughter's direction.

"I will not allow you to speak to her that way!" Tiara heard Stephanie say in her defense. "If you would have been a mother instead of a credit card user, then maybe none of this would have happened, bitch!"

"You're fired!" Cat countered, but Stephanie just laughed.

"We all know that when Blake died, he left everything to Vincent and Tiara. You can't fire shit!"

Tiara ignored their argument and ran up the stairs to her room. When she got there, she had a complete mental breakdown and fell to her knees. She did the only thing she had the energy to do; she cried, and she screamed. She cried for her father, she cried for Brandy, and she cried for the fact that the boy she had fallen in love with had betrayed her. Tiara had tried to call Mario many times, but his phone had been disconnected. She didn't know where he lived. In the months that they had spent talking and getting to know each other, she never inquired on where he lay his head at night. She felt like a fool, and she didn't have anything to live for anymore. She threw her hat and veil off of her head and fell to the floor crying in despair.

The images of Brandy and her father's dull eyes entered her head. Her heart wrenched. She felt like she didn't have the right to breathe the air she was breathing. Struggling to her feet, Tiara made her way to her panty drawer. From it, she pulled a small bottle of 1800 Tequila. Alcohol in hand, she went into the bathroom. Her eyesight was blurry, and she could barely see where she was going, but she knew what she was aiming for. When she was in the bathroom, she stared into the mirror on her medicine cabinet and saw the mascara running down her face. Her lips trembled when she looked at her own face. All she saw was her father.

"Fuck!" she screamed and punched the mirror. The glass shattered and blood from her wounded hand dripped into the sink. She ignored the pain in her hand and opened the cabinet looking for anything. Her hand fell on a bottle of Tylenol, and she popped open the top. She didn't use any water, just alcohol, and, she just took the whole bottle to the head and swallowed pill after pill until the bottle was empty.

It didn't take long for her to feel the drugs take effect. Tiara dropped to the ground and watched as the world faded around her. She was happy to leave a place where she had absolutely nothing. She was looking forward to joining Brandy and her father. The last thing she remembered was seeing Stephanie's plump frame entering her room and calling her name. When she saw Tiara lying on the ground and the open bottle of pills lying next to her, she screamed.

Chapter 12

Beep. Beep. Beep.

Cat listened to the machines hooked up to Tiara's still body. Her normally flawless face was plagued with sadness. The dark bags under her eyes gave away the fact that she hadn't been able to sleep in days. She was all cried out and couldn't even force another tear to come from her eyes. She watched the steadiness of Tiara's chest go up and down. Her own daughter had turned out to be a gift and a curse, and Cat didn't know how she was going to stomach it all.

It was true that Cat only gave birth to Tiara to make Blake happy. She had never really wanted a child. She knew she was too selfish, and she never wanted to have a kid that would potentially take the attention or the spotlight off of her. But she loved Blake, and she couldn't risk losing him over not giving him a baby. She was blessed to have found a man that could provide her with the life she always dreamt of, and if bearing one of his seeds was what she had to do to keep him, then it was a price she was willing to pay.

The first few months after having her, Cat woke up every day regretting her decision. She couldn't handle the sleepless nights and the constant breast-feeding, but she wanted to show Blake that she was capable of being a good mother and taking care of their new baby. Unfortunately for her, she was only able to keep up the façade for barely six months. Tiara stopped wanting to breast-feed, and Cat couldn't be happier. She hired Stephanie to come in and help her out part time. When she realized how much easier things were with a nanny, she asked Stephanie to work full time for her. Stephanie didn't mind the extra hours, and as time went on, she grew to love Tiara as if she were her own daughter.

For a while, Cat couldn't be happier with the way things were working out. She was able to go out and live her life without having to stay home because she had a built-in and qualified nanny that did everything for Tiara. She never regretted her actions because she genuinely loved her life. She was able to travel, buy anything her heart desired, and she had a seemingly endless supply of cash flow. Seeing how things were turning out in the long run, though, Cat was questioning if she'd made a mistake by having Stephanie do so much with Tiara. She barely knew her daughter, and her daughter practically hated her. Thinking back, she was regretting not spending time with Tiara to get to know her more and possibly even become friends with her. She could have made more of an effort to take Tiara on trips with her or even just take her out shopping at the mall.

Cat reached over and caressed her daughter's hand. She wished to God that she could take it all back and start over. Or if she could just take back what she did yesterday, she'd feel better. She didn't mean to come off so harsh when she yelled for someone to get Tiara out of the room. She was feeling overwhelmed with the crowd of people all around her, and she felt like she was about to lose her mind. When she saw Tiara looking at her from across the room, she saw so much of her husband Blake in Tiara that she just couldn't handle it. She knew she was wrong for what she did, and now, she was just praying that her daughter would pull through so she could try to start over with her.

It was hard for Cat to stomach all of the events that had happened in the last weeks. Tiara had been unconscious for three days. If Stephanie hadn't found her when she did, then Tiara would have already been dead. She couldn't help but wonder how she would have felt or what she would be doing right now if Stephanie had never gone up to check on her.

She wondered if she would be filled with grief beyond what she could manage and if she'd be getting ready to take her life too . . . . Or maybe things would have been better off. Tiara would no longer be suffering, and Cat would be able to start over. She felt a pang of guilt for even thinking that Tiara might be better off dead. She quickly tried to shake that thought out of her mind. Lying in that bed, Tiara looked so peaceful. Nothing like the angry girl she'd been over the last few months. Every time she looked into Tiara's face, she was instantly reminded of everything she wanted to forget.

At a time like this, she wished she had made an effort to make some friends instead of always being superficial with women she interacted with. For so long, she had focused so much on keeping up with her image and coming across a certain way to other women that she hadn't made any real friends. The reality of it was, with her husband gone, she was alone and had nobody to turn to. She couldn't even cry on her mother's shoulder because their relationship was even more strained than hers and Tiara's. She and her mother had barely spoken to each other in years. Of course, her mother called her as soon as she heard of Blake's death, but it was not to offer condolences. It was to tell her "I told you so." Cat's mother had never approved of her relationship with Blake. She was appalled at the fact that her daughter was running around with a "street thug," as she called him. She warned Cat about dating men like him before things got too serious between the couple; and when Cat told her about Blake's marriage proposal, she once again tried to be the voice of reason to her daughter. She knew ultimately it wouldn't end well. Things like that always ended the same. She asked her daughter if she was prepared to go to many funerals. But back then, Cat was so intrigued by the life that Blake lived that she would go to the moon and back for him. All she ever wanted was a strong, powerful, and rich man. In Blake, she got all three. She would not let that go.

As she sat there in the dim light of the hospital room, she wondered if she were to be given a do over, would she change anything. She looked at Tiara lying there helpless and broken. Guilt and sadness welled in Cat's chest because she knew what her answer was.

A knock at the door jarred her from her thoughts, and she was forced to look up at the door. There was a nice-looking woman standing in the entrance. She had spectacles sitting at the tip of her nose, and she smiled down at Cat's sad figure.

"Hello, Mrs. Rogers," she said softly. Her voice was sweeter than honey.

"Um," Cat's voice was barely louder than a whisper. She cleared her throat. "I'm sorry. Who are you?"

"I beg your pardon," the woman said. "My name is Clarice Chambers. I've come to you from the Elegant Juvenile Help Center. I wanted to speak to you about your daughter, Tiara Rogers."

"What about Tiara?" Cat looked behind her and saw two burly men in suits standing there.

"I have read up on your daughter's case, and we believe that our services will be very beneficial to her." Clarice focused her attention on the envelope she was carrying. Pushing her glasses up, she opened the folder. "Her records show that she was a troubled child in school, and she uses drugs for recreational purposes. I also understand that her father just passed?'"

She said it like a question, but her tone of voice let Cat know that she was already aware of the answer. Cat nodded her head and put her hand to her mouth.

"Don't cry, Mrs. Rogers. That is why we are here. We are here to help. With the services we provide, we will have her whipped back into shape in no time."

"What services are those exactly?" Cat asked cautiously.

"At the Elegant Juvenile Help Center, we have a variety of programs that I think would be beneficial to your daughter. We are fully staffed and offer round-the-clock supervision to ensure that our patients are safe and protected at all times. Whether they need protection from themselves or others." Clarice reached into her purse and handed Cat a pamphlet. "I am aware your daughter is in a very sensitive state right now, mentally as well as physically."

"Yes, she is." Cat looked over at her daughter and squeezed her hand. "She's been through a lot in the last couple of weeks," she said as a tear escaped her right eye.

"I understand, Mrs. Rogers." Clarice gave a warm smile. "I can assure you when your daughter wakes up, we will work diligently to get her back in top shape. We will provide her with one-on-one counseling services, as well as group therapy. Within our facility, we also have aerobics classes, yoga, and other physical recreational activities to keep patients active and healthy while they work on improving their minds and mental abilities. At our facility, we believe it is important for the mind, body, and soul to all be aligned." Clarice looked over at Cat who looked very deep in thought.

"If I was to agree to enroll her into the center, how long are you able to keep her?" Cat knew how the question must sound, but she was being honest. She heard everything the lady said, and it sounded like Tiara could really benefit from going to a center like that. She had been sitting in that room for hours thinking and trying to figure out what she was going to do with her daughter, and this lady walking into the hospital room was like a godsend to her. With Tiara being out of the house, it would give her time to figure out things for herself. As much as she loved her daughter, she still had mixed emotions toward her. She didn't know if she could handle being a single mother to Tiara now that Blake was gone. She didn't know the first thing about being a parent, especially a single one, and she knew Stephanie wasn't going to make things any easier for her. With Tiara being almost eighteen, if they could hold her until then, Cat would have more than enough time to sort things out. Then Tiara would be of age so she could decide for herself what she wanted to do too.

"We can keep her for however long you want," Clarice said and handed Cat a form. "All you have to do is sign here."

"Mmmm," Tiara moaned, suddenly feeling a pain shoot throughout her body. She tried to open her eyes, but it proved difficult. Her eyelids felt like they had rocks over them, and they had been shut for a long time. After numerous attempts, she was finally able to open them in a slit and view things. As she tried to look out, she couldn't make out anything of what she saw. It all looked like she was surrounded by a blurry, blue sea. Her hearing was off as well, and it felt like she was under water.

"Owwww!" she groaned again, trying to move her arms.

Her whole body ached when she moved at a snail's pace as she tried to sit upright. In the distance, she could here faint beeping sounds. When she was finally able to sit up, she regretted it. Her head throbbed, and she didn't know where she was. All around her, she heard all types of machines making sounds, but she still couldn't see anything too clearly.

"Take it easy, Tiara," she heard a familiar voice say. "You just came out of a coma."

"Mommy?" Tiara croaked. "Where am I?"

Tiara's eyes started to focus more, and she knew that the horrible nightmare she just had was not a nightmare after all.

"You're in the hospital." Cat came over to fluff her pillows and help Tiara lie back down.

"When can I go home?" Tiara asked. "I hate hospitals." Her throat felt dry, and she tried to clear it in hopes that it would help, but it only made it feel worse.

"Tiara," Cat sighed, trying to think of how she was going to tell her the news. "You won't be coming home with me today."

"Huh?" Tiara asked. "When can I go home then?"

"Um . . . I'm not sure, Tiara. It's probably going to be awhile." Cat's voice shook, and she took her seat once again beside the bed. "But you won't be coming home with me at all."

"What do you mean I won't be going home, Mom?" Tiara's heart began to thump powerfully. "That's my house. I live there!" Tiara tried her damnedest to raise her voice, but she could barely get it above a whisper.

"Not anymore, Tiara." Cat looked at her hands. "Not after everything. I can't have you there. You look too much like him. I can't bear to have you around me right now. I need to heal."

"*You* need to heal?" Tiara couldn't believe what her mother had just said. She felt a surge of anger come over her and found the strength to speak up to her mom. "And you don't think *I* need to heal too?"

"You tried to commit suicide, Tiara! What am I supposed to do with you doing something like that? Shit, I don't even know what I'm doing with myself right now," Cat yelled, making Tiara's headache worse. "You have taken everything away from me, and a part of me kind of wishes those pills would have worked and taken your life!" Cat's hand immediately flew to her mouth when she realized what she had just said.

"I knew it," Tiara fought back her sobs. "I knew you never loved me. The good thing is I'll be eighteen soon, and I won't need you. Shit, I don't even need you now. Get the fuck out of my room!"

"Tiara, I'm sorry," Cat said. "I do love you. I'm just going through a lot."

"Fuck you and fuck what you're going through," Tiara spat at her mother.

There was a long pause before Cat spoke again. "Someone came by here a few days ago from the Elegant Juvenile Help Center. You'll be going to stay with them for a while. I already signed the consent forms. They will be here when you are ready to be released. Since you are out of a coma, they will probably send somebody to speak with you soon."

"You signed your rights to me away? You bitch! How could you!" Tiara was in disbelief.

"I am sorry, Tiara," she said. "I really am."

"You're not sorry! You only care about yourself!" Tiara sat up and tried to pull all of the tubes from her body so she could move from her bed and get to her mother. "I hate you! I swear to God I fucking hate you!"

Cat could not take Tiara's screams. She stood up and held her hands up. The nurses had heard all the commotion and burst into the room. They ran past Cat to get to Tiara. Cat stood there bawling as two male nurses held Tiara down while the other jabbed a needle in her arm. The last image she would have of her daughter was of her head flopping to the side when the sedative kicked in.

When Tiara came to, she was being wheeled out of the hospital. Her eyes fluttered, and she heard the hazy voices of people around her. Then she heard the sound of doors opening and the sunlight hit her a second later. She clenched her eyes shut, and then eased them back open, trying to get her eyes to adjust to the light.

"Hey, she's awake," she heard a man's voice say.

She let her head fall to the right, and then to the left. She saw two men holding on to the sides of her bed as they pushed her to an awaiting van.

"W-where am I going?" she asked them.

"You, my dear," one of them grunted, "are going straight to hell. Doctor Pierce is going to love you."

Before Tiara could ask him what he meant by what he was saying, they pushed her up a ramp, into the back of a vehicle, and shut the doors behind her.

The first day at the Elegant Juvenile Help Center and Psychiatric Institution wasn't so bad for Tiara. The nurse, Clarice Chambers, checked all her vital signs and told Tiara that she would be able to walk by herself. She was prescribed some pain medicine and told her to wait for Doctor Pierce to come in and speak with her. She shut the door behind her and left Tiara alone in the room. She looked around from where she sat on the examining bed. It looked like any other doctor's office. She smiled while she reminisced about how she used to steal Band-Aids whenever Stephanie took her to the doctor when she was a little girl. Stephanie always made it a special day whenever Tiara had to go to the doctor to get shots or her regular physicals. She would always take Tiara out for ice cream afterward.

Thinking about her childhood brought a smile to her face, but it filled her heart with sadness at the same time. She wasn't a little girl anymore, and those happy days were long gone. Stephanie was gone, her father was gone, everything and everyone she ever knew was gone from her life. Just when she was about to burst out crying, there was a knock at the door signaling that the doctor had arrived.

"Come in," she said weakly.

A handsome man with straight white teeth and golden skin entered the room. He had a bald head and a thick, clean-shaven beard.

"Miss Tiara Rogers," he smiled at her kindly. "My name is Doctor Pierce."

"I know who you are," Tiara gulped.

Doctor Pierce's voice was pleasant enough; however, there was something about his presence that didn't sit right with Tiara. It was if he had a dark aura around him, and it made her squirm in her seat.

"No need to be nervous." Doctor Pierce saw Tiara's body stiffen as he approached and patted her knee. "We here at the Elegant Juvenile Help Center strive to assist in helping all of our guests feel special. I know you've had a tough past,

Tiara, and I know it's not easy to stomach the fact that you were sent here, but you don't have to worry. I don't feel like you're crazy or anything like that. I just think you need somebody to help you feel good, that's all."

He continued to talk to Tiara, patting her knee a few more times during the conversation before he told her that she would then be led to the room she would be staying in. She was informed that all of her things had been put there.

"OK," Tiara said, and before he could completely leave the room, she called him back. "Excuse me, Doctor Pierce?"

"Yes?"

"When will I be able to call home?" Tiara had no intentions to call home to speak to her mother. She actually wanted to call Stephanie.

"Unfortunately, your mother has put you on the no phone privilege list. You are not allowed to call home, or anywhere else, for that matter."

Why is that woman so determined to make me more miserable than I already am? Tiara felt a surge of hatred toward the woman who had given her life.

"Tiny will show you to your room," he told her and exited the room.

Tiny was a guard who was anything *but* that. He gripped Tiara's arm tightly as he led her through the hallways of the facility. When he finally reached the room that would be hers, he unlocked it and pushed her full force into the room. Before he slammed the door behind her, he eyed her lustfully. Tiara was on her knees and pushing herself back up, so she didn't even notice the man salivating over her.

"Hopefully, the doctor will allow me to sample you," Tiny whispered before shutting the door behind him. Tiara was too busy looking around the room and rubbing her knees to have paid attention to his comment.

The room felt cold and looked very dreary. There was a small lightbulb in the center of the ceiling which was the only source of light for the entire room. It wasn't a huge space, but that tiny lightbulb didn't do a very good job at lighting up the room. It wasn't very bright at all. Tiara looked around at the beds in the room before taking the one that did not seem to have an occupant. She busied herself by putting her things away and realized then that she didn't ask Doctor Pierce exactly what it was they did there for their patients. She'd read about facilities like this in her health class, though, and she hoped that she would be able to sit down and talk to a counselor about all of the things that were bottled up inside of her. She had also read in a blog before that sometimes it was beneficial to have a psychologist or therapist to talk to about your problems. Despite how things had gone down with her mom and how her mom had signed her into this facility, Tiara was trying her damnedest to look on the bright side of the situation. She was hoping that ultimately her coming here would turn out to be a positive thing and would help her in the long run.

She had just sat down on her bed and let the thought form in her mind when the door to her room opened and some men threw a girl on the bed beside her. When the doors shut again, Tiara studied the girl and took notice that she was very pretty. She had golden-brown skin and full mocha-colored lips. Her eyes were shaped like almonds, and her cheekbones were to die for. What Tiara also noticed was that the girl looked like she was high out of her mind.

Great, she thought, *they put me in the room with a crazy girl.*

The girl wiped the slobber from her mouth and rubbed her eyes. When she noticed Tiara sitting on the bed next to hers, she began to look around frantically. She looked over at Tiara and then glanced down at her belongings. Tiara felt sorry for the girl and how frightened she looked.

"You OK?" she asked. The girl nodded her head, but she didn't utter a single word.

Then as if the girl snapped out of her high trance, she reached down, grabbed her things, and clutched them close to her chest. Tiara was offended to see the girl grab her stuff like that. It was as if she thought Tiara was going to take something from her.

"Girl, ain't nobody trying to steal your stuff," she told the girl. "Where I'ma put it? We share the same room."

"Did I say you would?" the girl shot back checking inside of her bags. "Or do you just have a guilty conscience?"

"Well, you yanking your shit away like you got something I want." Tiara's voice dripped with irritation.

The girl turned her attention back to Tiara and studied her. "Why are you here?" the girl asked bluntly.

Tiara eyed her suspiciously, debating on whether she should tell this girl anything about herself. She had had a long day and wasn't sure she wanted to get into a conversation about all the shit she'd been going through. Add to that the fact that she was in no position to trust or want to get to know anyone new at this particular time in her life. Those that were supposed to be closest to her had betrayed and destroyed her trust. Her mother had literally signed her over to complete strangers, and her boyfriend had turned out to be an assassin. Here she was in a place that was damn near an asylum, sharing a room with a girl that, up until a minute ago, looked high as a kite. *Fuck it. I have nothing else to do,* Tiara thought when she finally decided to just talk to the girl and tell her the truth.

"My mom brought me here because she was tired of me," the new girl said just as Tiara was about to open her mouth to speak. "Said she couldn't put up with my shit anymore. I guess I wasn't the easiest bitch to get along with, but shit, I never thought she'd fuck me over like this. I don't think I would ever have the heart to do this to my child if I ever had one."

"I'm here for the same thing," Tiara said and lowered her head.

"Really?" the new girl sounded surprised.

"Yup, I . . ." Tiara said and then looked at her fingertips. "Well, I tried to kill myself, and when I woke up, I found out my mom had signed me over to come here."

"Why'd you try doing that to yourself?"

"Let me see how I can make my long story short," Tiara said as she put her thoughts together and tried to sum up everything that had transpired over the last month, "Some people tried to kill me and shot up my school some weeks back. Then my father was killed by taking a shot to the center of his head, and I was the one that found him. My mother hates me because she says I remind her too much of my father, and she also blames me for his death. Oh, and it turns out my boyfriend, the man I loved, was just using me the whole time and never loved me at all. The day my dad got buried, it all hit me at once, and I took some pills because I just didn't want to deal with any of it anymore. I just wanted to stop thinking about things, and I thought taking a bottle of pills would solve everything. I guess I was just tired of hurting all the time. My dad and I didn't have the best relationship, but we loved each other, and it all got to be too much for me. Shit got me all fucked up in the head, I guess." Tiara's voice was soft as she broke it down.

Tiara considered talking about Brandy's death but decided to leave that part out of the story. She honestly still wasn't ready to speak of her best friend's death. Just thinking about it had her throat tight. She had to shake Brandy's face from her mind. She also thought about talking a little more about Mario, but she changed her mind on that too.

"That's some fucked up shit," the girl said. "What's your name? I'm Elaya Elliot."

"My name is Tiara. Tiara Rogers," she said and leaned over so that she and Elaya could shake hands.

"How long have you been here?"

"I just got here today," Tiara answered. "How long you been here?"

"Almost three months," Elaya said.

"Does the time go slow or fast?"

"Some days go slow, and some go faster than others."

"Yeah, Doctor Pierce said as long as I follow his rules, then I won't have any problems."

"The rules are bullshit," Elaya said sadly. "Some sick bullshit."

"What do you mean? Doctor Pierce seemed cool. He looked like a regular doctor to me, I guess."

"Nah," Elaya said, rubbing her hands together. "Trust me. That nigga ain't cool at all."

"I feel like there's something that you aren't telling me," Tiara said, trying to see if she could get Elaya to open up more and explain what she meant about Doctor Pierce.

"Just be careful with him, Tee," was all Elaya said.

After that, Elaya stopped talking. She got on her bed and turned the other way. Tiara wanted to do the same thing, but her mind was running in different directions, and the last thing she wanted to do was sleep. She wouldn't be met with anything but nightmares anyway. Instead, she sighed and lay down on her back and tried to figure out how she'd gotten herself in the position she was in. How could she have not seen Mario for exactly what he had been? Why hadn't her parents let her date more so that she was able to tell the real from the fake? How could her mother really just write her off like she wasn't the one who pushed Tiara from her own body? Nothing made sense to her anymore, and the more she tried to understand it, the crazier she felt. Before finally deciding to get some sleep, she thought about what Elaya said and wondered what she meant by it.

Unfortunately for her, out of all her questions, the only one she'd get her answer to was the one about Doctor Pierce. It didn't take long for Tiara to figure out exactly what Elaya had meant by her statement. A few nights later, Tiara was woken up out of her sleep and literally dragged out of her bed and her room. She tried to focus on her surroundings, but everything was a blur. All she saw was the light in the long hallway and the two men half-dragging, half-carrying her.

"What's going on?" She tried to pull away.

"Shut up," one of their gruff voices said to her.

When they reached their destination, a room so dark that Tiara's eyes were having a tough time adjusting, she heard a man's voice say, "Thank you very much. Set her there and shut the door behind you."

Tiara felt the men lay her down on what seemed like a hospital bed; then she heard their footsteps exit the room. The lights suddenly were flicked on, and Tiara put her hands up and over her eyes to shield them from the light's brightness.

"My apologies, Tiara," she heard the same man's voice again. "I meant to do this earlier before you went to sleep, but I was wrapped up in meetings all day, and I won't be able to fit you in at all tomorrow, so this is the only time I have."

Tiara's eyes finally focused, and she looked at the owner of the voice. "Doctor Pierce?" she asked in a confused tone. "Why am I here? And why did those men drag me out of bed like I was some kind of animal?"

"I tell them to be careful with the new meat, but they never listen," he said, moving closer to her.

Tiara noticed that he was dressed casually in a navy-blue Ralph Lauren sweat suit, and she didn't like the look that was on his face. His smile was sly and sinister. She felt a knot form in the pit of her stomach causing her to become nauseated. She saw his eyes travel over her body hungrily, and her hands instantly clutched the end of her nightgown as she tried to pull it down low enough for it to cover her exposed legs.

"N-new meat?"

Doctor Pierce was so close to her that he could smell the vanilla from the lotion she applied to her body right after her shower earlier in the evening. The pointer finger on his right hand touched her face gently and traveled down to the area between her breasts. Tiara pulled away from him.

"Don't fight it," Doctor Pierce spoke softly and touched the softness of her hair. "You just may be the most beautiful girl I've ever seen. Nice full breasts."

He groped one of her breasts.

"Please stop," Tiara said, not believing what was happening. She tried to pull away, but that time he grabbed her by her neck.

"No! Don't touch me! Please!" Tiara said as she tried to push the doctor off of her.

"Aw," Doctor Pierce said. "And here I thought that you weren't going to be a fighter."

He slammed her down on the bed and reached back for something on the table behind him. Tiara tried to fight him off, but there was no point because he was stronger than she was. Her eyes bulged when she saw the syringe that he was holding in the air.

"Please don't," she tried to beg, but it came out as a croak.

Doctor Pierce didn't listen to her. All he could think of was how good her pussy was going to feel wrapped around him. He'd had her on his mind ever since he saw how thick she was on the first day they met.

"I'll let you in on some of the rules that the other girls have down pat," he grinned sinisterly at her. "First off, don't beg. It doesn't do anything but turn me on. If that's what you want, then by all means, beg daddy to stop. Second, once I start, I don't stop until I get what I want, so if you're a good girl and you follow instructions, it will be over faster than if you fight me. Last, the more you fight it, the more I will make it hurt. Well, hurt for you, of course. I'm going to enjoy myself regardless."

He jabbed the syringe in her neck and injected the drug. Tiara felt her body going limp until the only body part that she had control over was her eyes. Doctor Pierce smiled down at her and licked his lips. His hands traveled her body, and she felt it all; she just couldn't move to do anything about it. She felt his hands rubbing her thighs and squeezing them before he lifted her nightgown over her head.

He's going to rape me, Tiara thought, terrified. *Oh my God, he's going to rape me. He's a doctor, and he's about to rape me.*

Doctor Pierce unsnapped Tiara's bra and let her breasts fall freely. She heard a satisfied sound escape his mouth, and she felt his lips wrap around the areola of her left breast. He licked and sucked while his hand massaged the other. Tiara didn't know she was crying until she opened her eyes and felt the tears roll down the side of her face and into her ears. Doctor Pierce was mumbling on and on about how beautiful her body was and what a shame it was that she didn't appreciate it.

"I'm going to show you its true value, though," he said when he removed her underwear and opened her legs wide. "I'm going to make you feel real good even if you don't want it."

Doctor Pierce pulled his pants and his boxers down before he got on top of her. He kissed her neck and whispered things in her ear that were supposed to turn her on. Instead, he repulsed her, and the thought of him being inside of her was enough to make Tiara want to throw up. Doctor Pierce was handsome, but he would never have been somebody that Tiara opened her legs to willingly. He didn't even check to see if she was wet before he entered her. She grunted in pain as he pumped faster and harder. The last thing on his mind was taking it easy on her just because she was new. The whole time he stared at her face, taking pleasure in her discomfort. There was something about the way she had her face twisted up in agony that made him feel powerful. He loved how weak and limp she was. He could literally do anything he wanted to her at that moment. He was in control, and he loved it. He watched the way her breasts bounced every time he pounded into her and put one hand under her bare bottom and squeezed her cheek. He could tell that she wasn't a virgin, but her walls still clenched his shaft tightly. Doctor Pierce just couldn't believe that any of the girls truly *didn't* like what he did to them. Nonetheless, they all got wet for him. No lubricant was ever needed. He put his lips by Tiara's ear so that she would hear what he had to say.

"You're *my* property now, Tiara," he told her grinding into her slowly. "I own you because nobody wants you. You are my—fuck baby!" he had to pause because the feeling her pussy was giving him was too much at that moment. "This is my pussy, dammit! This is my fucking pussy, bitch. Whenever I want it and however I want it."

Tiara sobbed at his words and the fact that she felt every sensation from all of the things that he was doing to her. She screamed a horrible scream that nobody could hear because it was inside of her head. Her outer self was paralyzed. She felt lower than dirt, and she prayed that it would be over soon. Doctor Pierce licked her nipples and fucked her for the next ten minutes before he finally pulled out and released on the bed beneath her.

"I think I just fell in love with that pussy," he said, pulling Tiara's nightgown back down. "I need to get you on birth control soon. I want to hit this raw every time."

He patted Tiara's throbbing vagina softly before he went to notify the guards that it was time for them to take her back to her room.

"Don't worry," she heard Doctor Pierce say right before she was carried from the room, "the effects of the drug will wear off in just a few hours."

The men wearing the white scrubs carried her back to her room. Despite them knowing what had just happened to her, they didn't even have the decency to lay her gently on her bed. Instead, they tossed her on it like she was a piece of luggage. As soon as they were gone, Tiara started to groan loudly, trying to move her body, but it still wasn't in her control. She sobbed uncontrollably when the images of what had just happened to her flashed in her head. Then she felt a body join her in her bed, and if she could move, she would have flinched in surprise.

"Shhh," she heard Elaya's voice cooing. Elaya wrapped her arms around Tiara's body and held her. "He does it to me too. He's a sick monster. If I would have told you, you would have tried to run, and he would have hurt you ten times worse than this. I'm sorry, I'm so sorry, Tiara."

Tiara could tell by the tremble in Elaya's voice that she was crying too. Elaya hadn't even asked Tiara what had happened to her, but she didn't have to because she already knew. Doctor Pierce had done the same thing to her. Tiara understood then that she had been trying to warn her the first time they'd met.

How long has this been happening to you? Tiara wanted to ask, but her voice betrayed her. *You should have told me what was really going on here. We could have tried to run away together.* Her mind was racing with thoughts of things she wanted to say to Elaya, but unfortunately for her, it'd be awhile before she'd be able to speak again.

As the time passed and Tiara had more time to sort through her thoughts, she knew that even if Elaya had come right out and said that Doctor Pierce was a sick pervert who raped young girls, it wouldn't have changed anything. It wouldn't have helped her case in any way. Like Elaya said, she would have tried to run, and it would have happened anyway. It would have probably made things worse. Elaya stayed awake with Tiara until the drugs wore off. When they did, Tiara scooted away from Elaya and bunched up into a ball. Still, Elaya didn't move. She rubbed Tiara's back, soothing her nerves. She didn't have anybody there for her the first time Doctor Pierce violated her, so she wanted to be there for Tiara.

"I can't believe that just happened," Tiara whispered. "I can't believe any of this is happening. Why would my mother send me here? Why would she sign her rights over to this place?"

"I'm sure she doesn't know what kind of sick pervert Doctor Pierce is. Nobody does," Elaya said.

"We have to tell somebody," Tiara told her.

"Already thought of that," Elaya said sadly. "But Doctor Pierce is way too good at covering his tracks. He'll put a bunch of stuff in our records and make us out to seem like we are crazy and hallucinating. He'll have us looking like we made the whole shit up. Trust me, he already killed that bit of hope I had, and he'll kill yours too. The truth of the matter is, he's right. He owns us, and there ain't shit we can do about it. Who's going to believe us? We're juveniles, so that doesn't make us very credible. And who would we even tell in the first place? You act like we can just leave or make phone calls when we want."

"So what . . . We are just are supposed to deal with this shit?"

Elaya sighed and shrugged her shoulders. "What else can we do? We don't got nobody on the outside that cares about us. Plus, we ain't even got no way to get in contact with them if we did have somebody. Doctor Pierce knows what he's doing with every girl in this place."

Elaya felt bad that she was bursting Tiara's bubble, but she had been suffering in here long enough to know that there was no way out. When she first got raped, she was hopeful, like Tiara was right now. She sat there night after night putting different plans together on how she could somehow get out of the facility or how she could expose Doctor Pierce. But as time went on, she realized she was in a lose-lose situation no matter what. She had already tried to think of a way that she could escape, but none of her plans were foolproof, and they all led to dead ends. She wished that she could give Tiara hope, but she couldn't. There was nothing she could say that would make their situation any less grim than it already was. The only thing that she could promise Tiara was that it was going to get worse and more frequent, but she couldn't bring herself to say that out loud. For tonight, she felt it was best to just let Tiara get some rest.

"At least . . . At least we have each other now," was the best that Elaya could come up with.

Surprisingly, that sentence did seem to put Tiara at peace. "Thank you," she whispered.

Chapter 13

After Tiara's first "session" with Doctor Pierce he started seeing her more frequently; sometimes even three times a week. He told her that she just had a sexual aura about her, and he couldn't stay away. He said that women older than her would kill to have the ass and hips that she had. He drugged her up and did whatever he wanted to her body for hours at a time. The things he did to her made her hate herself. She hated the way her body reacted to the acts of cruelties. It got to the point where she couldn't even stomach to look at herself in the mirror. She never had an appetite but was forced to eat to maintain a certain weight that Doctor Pierce liked her at. Before she knew it, an entire month had passed, but it felt like an entire lifetime. She'd stopped crying herself to sleep only because being in her room with Elaya was the only part of the day she looked forward to. The two of them had many things in common, from their attitude all the way down to their tastes in music. Also, neither one of them could remember a time where they were truly happy.

During the day when Tiara wasn't talking to Elaya or in the library reading, she was listening to the chatter of the institution workers. She quickly figured out how Doctor Pierce was getting away with sexually assaulting almost every young girl there. He had all of his workers on payroll, and they were getting a lot of perks for keeping his dirty little secrets. She was just glad that she had Elaya there to keep her sane and together. They bonded through their suffering. They both felt like they were orphans, and they both hated their mothers. Despite what they were going through in the facility, they both had hopes and plans for their lives . . . if they ever made it out. They shared many of the same goals, and if you just sat in on a random conversation of theirs, you would never be able to guess that they were suffering or that they were going through their own personal hells from how they spoke so positively and confidently about their futures. The girls had learned to rely on and cope with each other to get them through their rough times.

One night, though, Tiara knew she had finally had enough when Elaya was thrown back in the room bleeding from between her thighs. Tiara threw herself on the floor where Elaya lay in a fetal position wearing nothing but her nightgown.

"It hurts, Ti Ti! It hurts so bad!"

"W-what did he do to you?" Tiara scooped Elaya's head up in her arms and held her head to her chest. "Oh my God, what did he do to you?"

"H-he put objects in me," Elaya sobbed. "And then he let the guards-he let the guards—"

"Shhhh," Tiara blinked, but it was no use. The tears poured from her eyes and down her cheeks. She already knew what had been done to Elaya, and it made her hold her friend tighter. "We gotta get out of here, Lay! We can't stay here another second. I can't go through that again. I can't even sleep without feeling his hands on me. Or seeing his face in the back of my eyelids. We *have* to get out of here."

"B-but how? If we run, they'll just bring us right back here."

"If we were able to get out of here they wouldn't be able to make us come back as long as we stay out long enough to turn eighteen. We'll be of age at that point, and eighteen-year-olds have to consent to be placed in something like this. We got put in here now because we were both still considered juveniles, and our parents had the right to sign off on it. But as soon as we turn eighteen, we have a choice, and there is nothing they can do about it."

"He won't let us leave. He would be too afraid of us talking about what goes on in here."

"That's why we have to kill him. He deserves to die."

Elaya heard the venom leaking from Tiara's voice and knew right then she was dead serious. She pulled away from Tiara's arms so that she could sit up. She ended up lying on her side due to the pain in her anus and vagina, but she was eager to hear what Tiara had to say.

"Okay, Ti Ti. What do we have to do? I'll do *anything* to get out of here."

"Anything?"

"Yes. I swear."

Tiara stood up and walked over to her bed.

"You know what Doctor Pierce has over us? The real reason why none of his patients have tried to leave?" She lifted up her mattress and grabbed something from under it. "Fear. He just *knows* we won't do anything. He targets women like us because he knows we are alone and don't have people on the outside looking out for us. We don't have anybody who would care enough to come looking. Look how long I've been here, and nobody has come to see me. Not even once.

And same thing for you. I haven't seen anybody come for you since I got here. Have you *ever* gotten any visitors?"

"No."

"Exactly. All we have is each other. And because of that, he tries to keep us both broken at the same time. Birds of a feather flock together. If you're down, then that means I'm down.

"But not anymore!"

She turned around to face Elaya once more and showed her what she had in her hands. Pens. But not just any pens. The plastic on these pens had been sharpened into what could be used as perfectly good shanks. The ink holders were still even in them, trimmed to an angle.

"How did you make these?" Elaya asked when Tiara sat back down beside her.

"With the razors Doctor Pierce gives me."

"He gives you razors?"

"Yea." Tiara didn't want to go into detail about how his sick ass liked when she didn't have any hair anywhere but on her head. "But listen, in a few hours, they're going to come get me for my 'session' with him. There are always two guards, have you noticed that? They have the master key, the key to get out of this place. So I have a plan on what we're going to do." Tiara smiled at her friend.

The next ten minutes she explained to Elaya what she had planned. After going over the plans, the girls took the next few hours to prepare. Elaya was sore, and her legs were hurting, but the desire to escape and get out of that hellhole was big enough to overpower the pain she felt. She knew she would run when it came time to do it. She packed her few belongings into her book bag and watched Tiara do the same. For the first time in a long time, Elaya felt hope. She said a silent prayer and asked God to help them get through their plans. She also took the time to thank God for bringing Tiara into her life. She was grateful to have a friend like her.

Chapter 14

"I wonder if he's going to let me fuck her this time." The guard Tiny was talking to another guard named Gil.

They were both big white men. Tiny had brown hair, and Gilbert was blond. They were two men that were friends outside of their work. The two of them had known each other for years, and they had both started working at the facility within weeks of each other. The fact that they were so big and ugly made it hard for them to get women, no matter what they did. However, when they landed the jobs of being Doctor Pierce's guards, they had access to an unlimited supply of pussy—every color and every size. It was safe to say that the men felt like they were in heaven. Women never willingly gave up their cookies, so it always felt good when they could take it. They got to stick their dicks into women that would never in their lifetime give them a second look in the real world. As if it wasn't bad enough that they were raping and abusing these women, the fact that they loved every second of it made their disgusting actions even worse. The two friends felt absolutely no remorse for what they were doing.

"Hell, no, you know she's his favorite."

"Well, I want some of her pussy. When he's done with her tonight, I think I'm going to make a quick little detour on the way back to her room."

"He'll kill you if he finds out."

"Key word, *if* he finds out," Tiny said, pulling a set of keys from his pocket.

He unlocked the door to the room and stepped into the darkness. The only light being given was from the moon shining through the one window that was in the room. Gil followed close behind him, and the two men went toward where Tiara was sleeping soundly in her bed. The covers were completely over her face like she was trying to hide.

"No point in trying to hide, Tiara," Tiny taunted. "It's playtime!"

He grabbed the cover and threw it back, and instantly, his eyes grew wide. There was nothing there but some pillows positioned like a body.

"What the fuck?" he said out loud.

"Where the fuck is she?" Gil asked as he looked around the room.

"Now!" the men heard a voice call out.

They started to turn around, but before they could, they both felt something cold and hard plunge in their necks. Blood spewed out everywhere as Tiara and Elaya repeatedly jabbed the shanks in and out of the guards' necks. The guards dropped to the ground, clutching their necks in hopes of being able to stop the gushes of blood from spilling out of them.

"G-get the keys, Lay!" Tiara whispered in a hurry.

"OK!" Elaya went to Tiny and pulled the keys from his hand and also the handgun from his waist. She did the same thing to Gil and handed a gun to Tiara.

Both girls were fully dressed in T-shirts and jeans with their backpacks on their backs.

"Come on, I know where he is. If he was expecting me, then there is only one place that he would be."

Tiara led the way to Doctor Pierce's office. The hallways were silent and empty, but still, the girls walked with precaution. The last thing they needed was to get caught before they even made it halfway out of the facility. They rounded a few more corners until finally, they reached their destination.

"His office?" Elaya asked peering down the hall at the office door that was slightly ajar.

"Yup." Tiara turned her nose up. She held her gun up and checked the clip like her father had taught her to do what seemed like so long ago. "Check the clip and make sure your safety is off."

"Girl, I don't know how to use these things. I have no idea what the hell you're talking about!" Elaya whispered frantically.

Tiara stopped and showed Elaya how to do it really quick before the two of them continued to ease their way down the hallway with their guns raised. When they got to the door, Tiara used her gun to push it open. She expected to see Doctor Pierce sitting at his desk waiting for her like he always was, but she was sadly mistaken. Instead, he had something up his sleeve for both of them. The moment that Tiara's outstretched arm entered the room, a hand grabbed her wrist and yanked her entire body all of the way into the room. She was spun around to face Elaya who was still in the hallway pointing her gun directly ahead.

Doctor Pierce used Tiara's own hand to aim the gun at her head and placed his free arm around her neck, squeezing tightly. He threw a wicked grin at Elaya and was openly delighted by the look of shock on her face.

"Did you two *really* think you would be able to sneak up on me and kill me? *Me?* You must have forgot that I have cameras in every hallway. I've been watching you since you left your room. Go on now, Elaya. Put the gun down, and I promise your punishment won't be as cruel as Tiara's."

"No! Elaya! Don't listen to him. If he kills me, so be it. You can still be free. Somebody needs to know about what goes on here!"

Elaya began to cry because the last thing she wanted to do was leave her friend behind. She shook her head.

"I'm not leaving you!"

Doctor Pierce jerked Tiara by the neck, causing her to choke and gasp for air.

"If you don't put the gun down in five seconds, it will be your fault that Tiara is dead. I'm going to put a bullet neatly in her temple; then *you* are going to take her place in my appointment book."

"I-it's fear, Elaya. It's just fear. Kill—"

"Five!" Doctor Pierce started counting as he cocked the pistol. "Four!"

"Tiara!"

"Kill him!"

"I don't have a shot!"

"Three! I am going to kill this bitch, Elaya! Put the fucking gun down, you worthless whore! Two!"

His words made Elaya's eyes flash hot. She aimed her gun just as he got to number "one" and took her shot.

Bot!

The gun in her hand went off and caught Doctor Pierce in the shoulder.

"Agh!" he grunted as he flew back, unwillingly letting Tiara go.

Tiara kneeled over and gasped for air. After taking a few deep breaths, she jumped forward toward Elaya. She snatched the gun from her and turned back to face Doctor Pierce who lay bleeding on the carpet in his spacious office. Walking back to him, she kicked his gun as far away from him as she could.

"You fucking piece of shit!" Tiara spewed her hate at him. "You took so much from me!" Tiara cried. "You stole from every girl in here!"

"Nobody wanted you," he said, clutching his left shoulder with his right hand. "You are all just throwaways."

"*I* wanted me! You were supposed to *help* me! You were supposed to help all of us! Now look at what the fuck you did!"

"Fuck you! I would do it all over again," he said and then licked his lips at her. "You will *always* be my favorite." He looked up at Tiara with a smug grin on his face.

Tiara wanted to wipe the look of glee from his face forever, and so she did. Her finger clicked on the trigger, and she released every bullet in the chamber in his face.

"You! Sick! Bastard!" She screamed and shot the gun until she no longer had any bullets left. "Ahhhh! I hate you, you son of a bitch!"

Although he was dead, she still kicked at his lifeless body. When she became tired of doing that, she spat at the dead doctor on the floor.

"Tiara!" Elaya said, grabbing her arm. "He's dead. He's dead!"

She gently touched Tiara on the shoulder and stared down at what was left of Doctor Pierce's face. She had never felt more relieved in her life. She and Tiara embraced for what seemed like forever and sobbed in each other's necks.

"It's over," Tiara whispered.

"It's finally over, Ti Ti," Elaya concurred and pulled back from her friend so that she could stare into her brown eyes. "We have to go. Grab that other gun and help me figure out how to delete these security videos."

The girls not only deleted the security videos, but they found a stash of sickening tapes that Doctor Pierce had. Apparently, he had been recording some of his "sessions" in that back room. There were about a dozen videotapes of him doing ungodly things to various patients. They found the ones that he'd recorded of them and deleted those too, but the others would be used as evidence. They sent copies of the videos to the police chief with an urgent 911 message and figured it was definitely time to get out of there.

It had been so long since Tiara had seen or smelled the air from the outside world. When she unlocked the main entrance door and felt that first gust of fresh air, she almost fell to the ground and kissed the concrete sidewalk. Elaya, who had been locked up far longer than she, actually did it. "Thank you, God!" she screamed over and over. "Oh my God! Thank you!"

Tiara hit the button on the car remote dangling from the keys she held and pointed them toward the parking lot in the front of the building. The lights of a small red Chevy Aveo blinked twice, and the girls ran thankfully toward it. Everything seemed so surreal, almost like a dream, and it didn't truly hit them that they were all the way free until they had gotten into the car and driven for a good ten minutes. They were excited to get as far away from that evil place as they could.

"Hey, Ti Ti, where are we going to go?"

Tiara didn't have an answer for her friend. She hadn't thought that far. Her attention was averted from Elaya for a second because there were sirens and lights flashing as police cars sped the other way. She smiled, knowing exactly where they were going. Then she glanced over at Elaya in the passenger seat and shrugged her shoulders.

"Shit, I don't know. Maybe a shelter or something? We can get jobs until we save up for a place. Then we can just live together and save money so we can figure out what we're gonna do. I don't know. The important thing right now is that we have each other. And we will be all right with just that for now."

Tiara meant every word she said, and she truly felt in her heart that as long as they had each other, they were going to be okay. She saw the silver lining through all of the bullshit she had just gone through. If she hadn't been brought to this godforsaken place, she would have never met Elaya. She would still be out there all alone. Tiara knew that she had found a friend for life in Elaya. She knew they had a true friendship that would last until they grew old and gray. Being able to just have somebody who genuinely loved her for her was enough to give her the strength to move forward in life. Separate, the two girls were like mud on a rainy day, but together, they flourished like the crops grown from it. Tiara was thankful to have someone like Elaya in her corner, someone who wanted to see her do well and pushed her to get there. What Doctor Pierce had done to them was horrible, but it wasn't the end of the world, and it was all over. The two ladies were free to go out and find the happiness that they deserved.

Chapter 15

Present Day

Tiara used her key to get into the secured entryway, and before she went up the three flights of stairs to her apartment, she checked her mail.

"Nothing but bills," she said to herself and sighed.

A&E helped fund her outlandish shopping addiction and kicking it with her friends while her job paid her bills. There was no extra money to live, like *really* live. She was almost twenty-two, and she knew it was time for her to make amends with the Rogers. She just didn't know when. She took the elevator all the way up to apartment number 313. Her apartment wasn't large and lavish the way she'd like it to be, but it was home, and she was proud of what she had.

She opened the door and threw the envelopes in her hand on the dining-room table.

Then she locked the door behind her and began to strip off her clothes right in the doorway. Tiara wanted nothing more than to take a long, hot shower in her bathroom. All the lights in her apartment were off, and she made her way through it naked and based off of memory. Undisturbed, she flicked on her light. Suddenly she screamed, long and loud.

"Oh, what?" the man sitting on her bed said, smiling at her. "You look like you've seen a ghost, my dear Tiara."

"W-what are you doing here?" Tiara stammered, covering her chest and her crotch with her hands.

"No point in covering up," the intruder said, eyeing Tiara's perfect body. "I've seen it all before. Tasted it all before. Fucked it all before."

"Leave!" Tiara yelled, looking around frantically before she finally located a pink silk Victoria's Secret robe and put it on. "Get out!"

Tiara regretted not having any sort of weapon on her, not even a stun gun. Her heart was pounding, and she couldn't deny that she was terrified. The man sitting on her queen-sized bed was the man who was responsible for her life being the way that it was. He had taken away her innocence at an early age and was responsible for hurting the people she held dearest to her heart.

"I'm afraid I can't do that," he said menacingly. His grin and the look in his eyes made her stomach drop. "You have a pretty high price on your head in the underworld."

He stood up from the bed, and Tiara took in his appearance. He was wearing a pair of 501 Levis and a Crooks and Castles sweatshirt, but tucked into his pants, Tiara took in the sight of the butt of a gun there. She backed herself into the farthest wall as he advanced on her. She prayed silently for herself and her best friends, hoping that they weren't next. Finally, he was directly in front of her, so close that she could smell the tacos he ate for lunch on his breath.

"Tiara Rogers," he said, using his pointer finger to gently brush against the cleavage showing through her robe, "responsible for the deaths of Blake Rogers and Doctor Pierce. How do you plea?"

"Fuck you," Tiara spat, realizing that she was going to die at the hands of the ingrate anyway. "You aren't even worthy to speak my name out loud."

"Worthy?" he said to her. "Do not forget that you spent a year being raped and molested by a man twice your age. You are nothing but a used-up whore."

His words cut Tiara deeply because she had spent the last three years working hard to heal and get past that part of her life. It was a daily struggle for her having to deal with the nightmares that presented themselves nightly. Every night she saw an image of Doctor Pierce on top of her, pounding into her relentlessly. She recalled the feelings of pleasure and hatred that seemed to intertwine together. She remembered the feeling of the drugs on the days she fought him off of her in the institute, and she often had flashbacks of the day three of his workers ran a train on her. What she was having a hard time understanding was how the man before her had even the slightest clue of what was going on in the clinic.

"Why are you here? What do you want from me?" Tiara did her best to sound confident. She refused to let him see that she was actually terrified inside. *Don't show him that you're scared. You've been through worse shit than this.* Tiara gave herself a little pep talk. She tried to mentally prepare herself for whatever was about to happen.

With one swift motion, he pulled out his gun and put it to her head. "This might just be one of the easiest hits that I've ever had to carry out since your father's," he said. "I just want you to know that back then, none of what I told you was a lie. You really were special to me. Now, it's just business."

At that moment his finger tightened around the trigger of his weapon and right before the shot rang out that would end her life, Tiara closed her eyes and took a deep breath when she felt the cold steel metal push against her temple. She had no regrets, so as she stood there vulnerable and unarmed, she prepared herself to die. She knew death would be coming for her one day. She wasn't expecting it to come to her so soon, but either way, here it was. Her mind rewound all the way back to the beginning of it all . . .

As she said her final prayer, she was startled when Mario pulled the pressure of the gun off of the side of her head.

"You know what? I have something even better for you," he said. "I want to enjoy that special goodness you have between your legs. I know it won't be as good as when I took your virginity all those years ago, but that's OK. Let's get those clothes off of you."

"No!" Tiara screamed and tried to run out of the room, but he grabbed her up in one swift motion. "Please, Mario! No," she pleaded with him.

"Oh, what? You can give it up to the doctor but not your ex-boyfriend?"

Tiara used her elbow to strike Mario in the mouth and ran out of the room. The house was dark, so it was hard to run anywhere without stumbling. Her heart was beating fast, and she knew that all she needed to do was get to the kitchen. She knew the front door wasn't an option, there were too many stairs to go down, and she didn't have time to wait for an elevator. She would have to kill him. The kitchen knives she owned were very sharp, and she wouldn't need much force behind them to dig deeply into his flesh.

"Umph!" Tiara yelled when she tripped over a chair in her dining room. Before she could get back on her feet and into the kitchen, she felt strong arms wrapping around her torso.

"Where do you think you're going?" Mario grunted trying to hold her steady. "You're a fighter, aren't you?"

As he carried her back toward her bedroom, Tiara held on to the door frame. Mario tried to pull her back into the bedroom. She looked back toward the room and instead of seeing her room, a room that she considered her sanctuary, she saw hell's flames. She used all the strength she had to hold on. She wouldn't give in and let him take her back there to be taken advantage of. She wouldn't let him abuse her body. But Mario pulled with all his might and finally got her to loosen her grip.

"Get the fuck off of me! Fuck you!" Tiara screamed, swinging her fists wildly.

"Fuck me?" Mario ducked her punches. "Aw, baby, I would love for you to."

He sent a left hook her way and connected with her temple. She was no match for the force that his fist presented her with. She fell limp in his arms. He had knocked her out cold. Mario dragged her back into her bedroom and began undressing her slowly. She felt herself going in and out of consciousness and began having flashbacks to her sessions with Doctor Pierce at the institution. She no longer saw Mario on top of her; instead, she saw Doctor Pierce. Tears rolled down her face as she remembered all the things she'd been going to counseling to forget. Everything was coming back to her, and her mind was flooding with all of the thoughts and images. The syringes, the feeling of his tongue all over her body. When Doctor Pierce raped her, he didn't use the same type of sedative that the other girls got. Tiara never learned the name of the drug he was using on her. All she knew was that it made her immobile, but she could still see and feel everything the sicko doctor did to her. The drug made her get wet, and it made her have more orgasms than she could remember, and he relished in it. He often would just watch her face to see her reactions to the things he did to her. He loved how thick she was and said often that they could tell she was black by how phat her ass was.

Doctor Pierce's favorite position was when she lay on her back on the examining table. He would spread her legs as wide as they could go so that he could see his dick entering and exiting her. He never waited for her to get wet because when he started plummeting her, her juices would automatically start to flow out of her. He said he loved the feeling of when her juices first started to flow.

"Your mind might not like this dick, but your body sure does," he would whisper in her ear during each session.

Tiara snapped back into reality and saw Mario fumbling with his belt buckle.

"'How did you find me?" she whispered. "How do you know about what I've been through?"

"What?" Mario said, ripping Tiara's blouse and bra, freeing her breasts. He gripped one breast in each hand. "Your mother, of course," he said. "She knew the whole time what was going on and what was happening in that institution. There were rumors about that place, but nobody could ever prove it. She heard about all of it. She knew. She felt like you deserved it."

More tears escaped her eyes when she felt Mario's hot mouth circle around the areola of her left breast. He sucked roughly and grinded his hardness against her opened legs. She gasped in pain.

"B-But," Tiara said, trying to ignore what he was doing to her, "m-my mother hates you." She tried to find her happy place. It was what she used to do whenever Doctor Pierce was violating her.

"Ahh," Mario smiled up at her and kissed her chin. "You would think so, right? Since I offed your father, I have gotten a pretty decent position as a top assassin in the underground. Your mother has long since forgotten about your father. She is now on the arm of your cousin Vincent."

"She wouldn't do that to my dad." Tiara choked back her tears. "She wouldn't."

"But she would," Mario whispered in a sing-song voice. "They're the ones who ordered this hit."

"You're lying. Cousin Vincent loves me," Tiara said, not wanting to believe anything Mario was saying. Her head still throbbed, and she didn't have the strength to push him off of her. "If anybody loves me, I know he does. He would h-have saved me if my mother told him where I was that whole time."

"I'm sure he does love you, but he loves money more," Mario said, wiggling his pants down. "He knew where you were the whole time. He knew all the shit that was going on in there too. He knew what Doctor Pierce was doing to you. He didn't give a fuck because with you gone, he had access to all of Blake's money for himself. He didn't have to share it with you."

Mario rose up off of Tiara and backhanded her across the face for good measure, just to make sure she was still unable to move. He tugged her bottoms off and moved her panties to the side.

"Phat like I remember it; a little tainted, though. But still edible."

He licked and sucked on Tiara's clit until she sobbed. Tiara tasted so sweet, and he was sad that he would have to kill her. He'd had many different kinds of pussies since her, but she was still the best.

"You must have been eating pineapples," Mario muttered licking and smacking his lips. He then looked up at Tiara who was staring hatefully back at him. He smiled and blew a kiss at her. "Anyway, back to what I was saying. Oh yeah, with you gone, he would have all of Blake's money to himself. But when Blake's amended will surfaced, it came to light that Blake had actually left everything to you. All of his assets were seized from Vincent, and all of his accounts were frozen until either you resurfaced or you died. Vincent sent an army for you at that institute you were in; imagine his frustration when he found out you had escaped."

Mario kissed her opening one more time before standing up and pulling Tiara to the end of the bed. He flipped her over and slammed her on her stomach with her legs dangling off of the bed. His hand cupped the back of her neck, while the other ripped off her panties.

"Your ass is still phat," Mario said. "Glad you didn't go into a crazy depression and starve yourself."

Tiara heard him spit. She knew what was about to happen. She squeezed her eyes shut and imagined being anywhere but there. She decided to focus on what Mario was saying to her to keep herself distracted from what was physically happening.

"Anyway," Mario said, "he thought that place would kill you, but it didn't. Without a legit death certificate, your mother and Vincent's money started running short. And that's where I come in. You have $2 million on your head. I plan on bringing it in and cashing out. I've been tailing you for months. You're so wrapped up in your own shit you didn't even notice."

Without warning, he thrust his dick so forcefully into her ass that she screamed. He pushed her head into the comforter so hard that she couldn't breathe. Then he pumped relentlessly and moaned in pleasure. Flashbacks of Doctor Pierce, Brandy's death, and how disappointed her father would be if he were to see her now plagued Tiara's mind. She had never done anything but cause people sorrow. Maybe her destiny was to live painfully and die the same way. Maybe it was time to accept her fate. Right before he was about to climax, Tiara felt the pressure lessen on her neck and heard the sound of a gun cock behind her.

"I gave your father the choice of having last words," he hissed and pulled his dick out of her ass, panting heavily. His nut blew everywhere, but he didn't care while he aimed the gun at the back of her head. "But you won't get that pleasure."

Bang!

When the shot rang out, Tiara tensed up, waiting for the pain to come . . . but it never came. Instead, she felt the weight of Mario's body fall on top of her. She looked over her shoulder and saw that the back of Mario's head had been blown off. She squealed and pushed him off of her as best as she could. Her body felt completely limp, and she was weak.

"Are you all right, ma?"

The voice caught her off guard, but she was relieved when she saw Stevelle standing there, holding a smoking gun. She smiled through her tears and nodded her head. She had never been happier to see Stevelle in her life. He was an absolute godsend. She felt in her heart he was meant to save her in that moment and in that exact situation.

"I saw a man sitting in his car and scoping you out outside of the baby shower. I was about to pull off, but something about him gave me a bad vibe, so I stayed back and decided to wait and watch for a little bit. I knew you were still waiting for your Uber, so I figured I'd sit around and make sure everything was all right with you. I saw when your ride got there. You got into a car, and as soon as you pulled off, so did he." He walked over to where she was lying on the ground so that he could help her up. "I'm sorry it took me so long to get up here. The man downstairs wasn't trying to let me through."

He pulled Tiara away from Mario's corpse, and without warning, she staggered to her feet and wrapped her arms tightly around his neck, not caring that she didn't have clothes on.

"Thank you," she barely could whisper. "Thank you so much."

He gently put his strong arms around her too and spoke into her hair. "I think we need to get you to a hospital, baby girl. We should have you looked at and make sure you're okay."

"No, thank you," Tiara said as she lowered her head and looked toward the ground, "I'm OK. I've been through a lot worse."

Stevelle helped Tiara walk to the living room. He turned on a lamp and sat her down gently on the plush couch. He sat beside her and examined her bruised face. He tried to keep his face as expressionless as possible, not wanting to make her feel any worse than she already did. Unknown to her, he knew all about her past. He and Clarence had been boys for a long time, and Clarence had told him what Elaya and Tiara had gone through while they were in the juvenile facility. When Clarence started dating Elaya, she always seemed to flinch and tense up whenever they would start kissing or if he tried to cop a feel. At first, he tried to ignore it, but eventually, he couldn't help but to take it personal. One day, he finally confronted Elaya and asked her why she acted like that, and Elaya spilled her heart out to him and revealed everything that had happened to her and Tiara.

When Stevelle saw Tiara, he immediately remembered her from when they were back in high school. He had always like her and felt there was something special about her, but back then, he didn't have the guts to approach her. After Stevelle told his boy Clarence about liking Tiara, Clarence told him everything he knew about the girls. He didn't tell him as a way to talk shit about their issues or to make it seem like a girl like Tiara was damaged goods, but because he knew it wasn't easy being with a girl with a past like that. Any other man would run the other way after hearing all of that, but not Stevelle. He looked at Tiara and still saw something special in her. Even with her being as broken as she was, he knew she wasn't like the rest of the girls out here. When he approached her at the baby shower and they started talking, he felt a spark that he had been missing out on with every other girl he'd messed around with.

Now, as she sat there before him all battered and bruised, he felt a sense of guilt because he hadn't been able to get there sooner to protect her. Instinctively, he put his hand to her cheek. He wanted to blow his own brains out for not getting up the stairs faster. If only he had pushed harder and convinced her to chill with him after the baby shower, they could have gone somewhere instead of her going home.

"It's not your fault," Tiara told him, putting her hand on his. She'd seen the look of guilt cross his face, and she wanted him to know that she didn't blame him. "If you hadn't come when you did, I wouldn't even be here."

"I'm sorry, Tiara," was all he could say as he gazed into her eyes.

"No, really," Tiara said as she squeezed his hand. "You don't need to apologize. If anything, *I'm* sorry. I feel terrible that you just got dragged into something that has nothing to do with you."

"Nah, it's cool," Stevelle said, feeling a little bit better. "It's over now. I'm glad you're okay."

Listening to his words, she wished to God what he said really was true, but she knew it wasn't. Unfortunately, for her, the nightmare was far from over. As much as she would have liked to talk more with Stevelle, she felt too numb to say anything else. Instead, she leaned into his warm hand and closed her eyes for a little bit, trying to get rid of the creepy, crawly feeling that was lingering on her skin. She tried to wrap her mind around the fact that she had just been raped—again.

"Can you stand up?" he asked.

She nodded and stood up to try her legs. They were still so weak that she fell right back down.

"Hold on," he told her. He disappeared for a second, and shortly after, she heard water running in her bathroom. Tiara did her best to keep her eyes off of Mario's body. Even though she knew he was dead, she felt like his soul was lingering in the room. She felt chills throughout her body and jumped when Stevelle came back to the room and touched her shoulder.

"It's just me," he said and scooped her up into his arms. "I won't let anyone hurt you again. Come on."

He carried her all the way to the bathroom and set her down on the counter. The water in the tub was still running, and the bubbles were already fizzing.

"I don't want you to have to go back into that room," Stevelle told her. "Tell me where your clothes are, and I'll grab them for you. Get in the tub."

She told him where he could find a Victoria's Secret Pink outfit, her underwear, socks, and a pair of all-white Nike Air Maxes. When he came back, she was already in the tub and had turned the water off. The bubbles covered her entire body, and the only thing that Stevelle was able to see were her shoulders. He placed her clothes on the counter and her shoes next to the toilet.

"I hit my nigga up. He's on his way so that we can get rid of this body. Take all the time you need."

There was something about the smoothness in his voice that made her feel at peace. She could feel her body relax, and she closed her eyes, allowing the warmth of the water to help ease the aches and pains she had throughout her body. It felt great for her to be immersed in the hot water. When the door shut behind him, she leaned back and tried to relax a little bit. All she had wanted to do was bathe and clear her mind. She thought about what the counselor was always telling her: to let go of her past and just put it behind her. She deemed it right then as bullshit. There was no putting what she had been through behind her. It always popped back up at the worst times. She had to face all of her problems head-on because even though they were the things that had caused her the most pain, they were also what helped her build the strongest of skins. She stayed there in that tub for a little over an hour, running more hot water once it started to get cold.

When she got out of the tub, she stood naked in front of the mirror and wiped her hand across it. She stared into it and saw a girl who had once been so beautiful and innocent. She saw the girl who swallowed a bottle of pills, but she also saw the *woman* who had gotten through it all and had been able to build herself and her life practically out of nothing. She and her best friend had been mentally and physically destroyed, yet, they were able to heal and move forward. They both were still standing, and she refused to continue to let the past haunt her. She was ready to come into a new season of her life. And the first step was for her to stop trying to run from her past and just confront it head-on.

She got dressed, brushed her hair neatly into a bun at the top of her head, and treated some of the cuts on her cheek. When she heard a knock on the door, she opened it to see Stevelle standing there.

"Well, look who's awake," Stevelle spoke softly. "Can I come in?"

She stepped aside so he could enter.

"Did you have a good bath?"

"How long was I in there?" she asked.

"For a minute."

"I'm sorry," Tiara said. "I didn't mean to hold you up like this."

"Nah, it's cool. I don't mind," he said, enjoying the fact that she seemed so comfortable with him.

"So who was he?" Pulling Tiara into his chest, Stevelle gently pushed her hair to the side so he could speak into her ear.

"My ex-boyfriend from back in high school," Tiara told him. "He's the one responsible for my father's death. I thought—no—I was *stupid* enough to think that he loved me. But it was just a setup to get close to my father. He killed him, and it's all my fault."

"Nah," Stevelle shook his head. "Your pops' death is not on your hands. Don't say no stupid shit like that. This game is live or die. Everybody knows the price that you could possibly pay just by rolling the dice. You were young back then. And niggas know how to get exactly what they want. He cased you and fed you all the bullshit he knew that you wanted to hear."

"Exactly. I fell for it, and that makes me stupid."

"Nah, that makes you a genuine person. It's not your fault that you expected the same in return."

"My daddy called me green," Tiara said, thinking back to the time that she walked into the house and spent the evening talking with her dad. "And back then, I was. I thought I'd gotten better. I didn't think I would have to watch my back anymore. But at the end of the day, I am a Rogers, and I know now that I will never be able to run from that. I don't know if you know anything about who my family is, but—"

"I know who your father was, Tiara," Stevelle interjected.

Stevelle wanted to ask her a question but changed his mind when the question was at the tip of his tongue. He would let her tell him about her past on her own time. The last thing he wanted to do was pry. He opted to ask her something else, though.

"Why was he here? If he killed your pops, that means he got what he wanted, right? After all this time, what would make him come back for you?"

Suddenly, Mario's words replayed over in her head, and Tiara's blood ran cold. Her eyes opened up like saucers, and she looked into Stevelle's worried face.

"He told me . . . He told me that my mother and my cousin Vincent sent him to kill me," Tiara whispered. "She's the one who signed me away and had me put into the facility with Elaya." She stopped speaking to catch her breath. She felt a rush of anxiety come over her as everything Mario had said was coming back to her. She took another breath before she tried to speak again. "And I don't know how he found me. But now I know that they won't stop until I'm dead. The thing is, my father left everything he ever owned to me. With me out of the picture I thought it had all gone to my cousin Vincent, but apparently, that's not the case. Unless I'm dead, they can't touch any of it; which explains why they're after me."

"Shit," Stevelle said, now understanding the severity of the situation.

He knew exactly who Vincent Rogers was. Ever since Blake had been killed, he'd been running the streets loosely. He wasn't quite the business-man that Blake was and couldn't be if he tried. No longer was the Rogers's name connected with being the head of streets. Vincent had bowed to Rodriguez, and because of him, the entire Rogers's estate was in debt. He had been Blake's right-hand man; however, he was more of an accountant than a drug dealer. He didn't know the first thing about flipping work the way that it was supposed to be flipped. It all was beginning to make sense why he wanted his niece dead. If Blake Rogers's whole estate was left to Tiara, that meant she was caked up—*beyond* caked up. He glanced around her tiny apartment and back at her. She deserved so much more than that. She deserved the millions that she had waiting for her.

"So if your dad left everything to you, why haven't you gone to a lawyer and taken it?" he asked.

"Because it's not worth it to me."

For the next thirty minutes, he sat there and listened to her talk about her goals and what she wanted for herself. After hearing that she had been brought up with security, a cleaning staff, and her own personal nanny, he was surprised that she didn't turn out to be an uptight woman. She was actually very humble and somebody who put her best foot forward. For some reason, she kept getting knocked down, but something in him wanted to be the one to pick her up this time.

"No!" Tiara exclaimed. "It is too dangerous. I don't want you getting hurt because of me."

Stevelle took both of her hands in his and put his forehead on hers. "Listen, shorty, this ain't up for debate. You might not have seen me or known me back in high school because I was too busy putting in work. I've been working for a long time, and my ranks have come up quite nicely in the streets. Ever since your father died, it's pretty much been eat or be eaten in the streets, and believe me, I've been eating. I got my own little crew. We ain't no cartel or nothing, but we gets down. Just say the word and we on they asses."

Tiara gave a weak smile and removed her hands from his. She shook her head sadly and looked up at him. This man barely even knew her but was willing to go out on a limb and help her in her situation. The only thing he could say about her was that she was pretty and that he wanted to take her out. She felt embarrassed that he had witnessed another man inside of her. Her emotions were all over the place. She felt sad, angry, embarrassed, and confused about what to do. This man had saved her, and she would forever be grateful. As good as his offer sounded, she wouldn't accept it. She couldn't risk another life being taken because of her. Too many people had died already, and she didn't think she could handle seeing someone die just because they had the misfortune of knowing her.

"Thank you for what you did for me tonight, but I can't accept your offer," she told him. "I can't ask you to go to war behind me. You can leave now."

"Why not? And you never asked me for anything. This is all *my* idea. This is all *my* doing. I'm just a man trying to do what's right."

"How do you know this is right? This will start a whole new war. Not just with the Rogers, but Rodriguez will come after us too. Just like they did my daddy. I don't know how many people my cousin has at this point, and I don't know too much about Rodriguez, but if he was bold enough to go after my father, he must have a pretty strong army behind him. If you really only have a small crew, then we are already outnumbered."

"One, don't underestimate my niggas. We're as gutter as they come. This pack of wolves has entered a lion's den and came out victorious, you feel me? Two, you ain't really got a choice. After seeing the shit that went down tonight, ain't no way I'ma leave you wide open. I'll kill a mothafucka who even thinks he can come close to you." His deep voice boomed and made Tiara's lip quiver.

"But . . . But why? Why are you willing to do all of that for me?"

"Because I see something in you." Stevelle shrugged. "People done hurt you all your life. My granny always tells me that hurt people, hurt people. But now that I've met you, I don't think that's too true anymore. And plus, you owe me a date. I can't take you out if you're dead."

***

After a while, he left her in the bathroom so she could take care of some of the bruises on her face, and he went into the living room. As she took a step forward, she heard voices that she didn't recognize.

"I paid that nigga downstairs five Gs to keep him quiet," she heard a male voice say. "I grabbed all the security cameras too."

"Cool," Stevelle responded. "But it don't even matter. She ain't never coming back here anyway."

"You gon' take her to your spot?"

"Yeah, for now."

"Man, that's Blake Rogers's daughter for real, bruh?" a new voice said, that one a female.

"Yeah," Stevelle said.

"A'ight," the woman said. "Blake helped my family out a lot back in the day. His mom and my granny was real cool peoples growing up. As a kid, I never wanted for anything. That nigga had gwap for days and always laced my granny. I don't get it, though. Can you please tell me why the fuck Blake Rogers's daughter is living in a place like this? This whole apartment should be the size of her room."

Tiara turned off the bathroom light but remained standing in the doorway, wanting to hear what Stevelle would say next as his response. Although she had been content in her apartment, the girl was right. Tiara's room at her father's house was way bigger. She guessed after being cramped in that room at the facility with Elaya, anything was better than that.

"They stripped her of her crown," Stevelle replied. "And to keep it a buck fifty with y'all, I ain't just call you here to move a dead body. I called y'all here because I need you to help me help her get it back."

Tiara held her breath, waiting for a sudden uproar of protests. She was sure his people would keep it real with him. She was positive they would tell him he was stupid for offering to help a girl he barely knew and that what he was saying was crazy. She just knew they were going to tell him he was out of his mind.

"A'ight, I'm down," the man's voice said.

"Aye!" the girl said, sounding like she'd just had a revelation. "Nigga, she can make us her personal bodyguards!"

Tiara stifled a laugh and put her hand to her mouth, but it was too late. They had heard her. Stevelle came around the corner and looked down the small hallway to where she stood.

"Eavesdropping?"

"Y'all was talking about me," Tiara told him. "I don't think that qualifies as eavesdropping."

"Come in here," he grinned at her. "Come meet a couple of my peoples."

She followed him back into the living room, glancing toward her bedroom where Mario's body had been. It was gone, and the only thing that remained was a small pool of blood.

"This my nigga Keys," he said, nodding toward the female. "She's the realest in the game, I promise. A mean-ass shot too."

Tiara hid her shock. The woman he pointed to looked more like a nigga than some of these "real" dudes that she'd see out in the streets.

Keys's hair was styled in a fade, with braids and a small bun at the top of her head. She was light skinned with hazel-colored eyes and freckles sprinkled neatly across her button nose. She rocked an all-white fitted True Religion hoodie, light blue jeans, and a pair of Legend Blue Jordan 11s on her feet.

"What's good, shorty?" Keys smiled and nodded her head at Tiara. "I heard that nigga tried to come in and off you. Glad my bro got here when he could. These niggas don't respect royalty these days."

Tiara returned her smile, and Stevelle pointed at the other person in the room.

"And this is Mook."

Mook was as tall as Stevelle but way bigger in weight. He wasn't fat at all, though. He looked like he was made of solid muscle. You could tell this guy could probably knock anybody out with just half of a punch. He too wore a hoodie. His was black, with a pair of tan pants and a pair of all-black Huaraches. Mook stepped forward and kissed her hand in greeting.

"Nice to meet you, Princess."

It had been so long since somebody called her that to her face that she was taken aback. She let his hand go and looked back and forth from him to Keys. Naturally, her eyebrows raised curiously. Mook and Keys were dressed to the nines and looked clean and fresh like they had just come to the house to kick it and that's it.

"If y'all moved that body why isn't there any blood on you?"

The three people before her looked at each other before bursting out laughing in unison. Keys shrugged her shoulders at Tiara, still grinning.

"We're professionals, baby," she said. "This a brand-new hoodie. Shit cost me a stack. I wasn't about to let a fuck boy ruin my shit. We wrapped that nigga up tight. That nigga finna be at the bottom of the Trinity swimming with the fishes."

"Thank you," Tiara told them. "Nah, for real, thank you. But I overheard y'all. Why are you all willing to help me? You all don't know me from a hole in the wall."

Mook grabbed a black fitted hat from off of Tiara's couch and placed it over the waves on his head. "You might not have known it, but you got people in these streets," he said. "We been here the whole time. We just ain't know where you were."

"Yeah," Keys spoke up, putting her hood over her head. "Your pops did a lot for the people in the hood. He helped a lot of our families out here. We wouldn't have shit if it wasn't for him.

He paid everybody on our block's mortgages off so we could really say we owned the block. Them white people couldn't fuck with us after that. He was a real nigga, man. The least we can do is make sure his seed is straight. Plus, you gon' make us your bodyguards, right? When we put you back up on your throne."

Hearing the things about her father that she didn't know made Tiara feel good inside but also made her see that she had never truly known who he was. He told her a long time ago that one day she'd have the choice to take his place. The person sitting in his seat may have been a Rogers, but it wasn't the right one. It was Tiara that had his blood running through her veins. She held her hand out for Keys to shake.

"If you help me get my daddy's empire back, you can have anything you want."

"You got it, baby girl. That's a done deal." Keys shook hands with Tiara. Tiara was excited and anxious for what was to come.

It's time for me to take back what's mine.

Chapter 16

After they left Tiara's house, Stevelle drove her forty-five minutes away to Anex Avenue where his condo was. He led her to his guest bedroom and told her to make herself at home. Then he told her to go to sleep and that he would talk more about their next moves in the morning. To that, Tiara had no argument. She was dead tired and was asleep before her head even hit the pillow.

When she woke up the next morning, she thought everything that had happened the night before had all been a bad dream. However, the soft, queen-sized bed and navy-blue comforter that she was wrapped in quickly reminded her that she was in Stevelle's guest room. Everything had all been real. She squinted her sleepy eyes and looked around the room. The sun's rays were shining through the window, so everything was visible without the overhead light. The walls in the room were cocaine white with a few paintings on them. To her left was a tall dresser, and in front of the bed was a wide dresser with a round mirror. Above the wide dresser was a flat-screen TV mounted on the wall. It had to have been at least sixty inches. The room was very spacious, and the closet was a walk-in. She assumed the bathroom was in the hallway because it wasn't in the room.

"Mmm," she moaned to herself and sat up so that she could stretch her arms wide. "Ahh!"

Her body was still extremely sore, and she had just reminded every nerve in it. Her joints were screaming angrily at her.

"Once you start moving around it won't hurt so bad." Stevelle entered the room carrying a plate of food. "You hungry? I made you some food."

"What kind of food?" Tiara looked at the plate in his hands skeptically.

Seeing how she was looking, Stevelle smirked because she didn't know that he was a man of many talents. Since he was the oldest of three, he often had to make sure his younger siblings were straight. His grandmother taught him how to make it do what it do in the kitchen. He knew how to cook so many dishes that he could make a cookbook if he wanted to.

"Don't look surprised like that, shorty," he said, handing her the plate. "I ain't gon feed you no bullshit, believe that."

On the plate were two pancakes made from scratch, hash browns made from scratch, bacon, and scrambled eggs with cheese on top.

"You ain't make this," Tiara said, snatching up the fork and digging in. She didn't realize how hungry she was until she started eating. "Mmm, this is good!"

"I damn sure did make it," Stevelle said, pleased watching her stuff her face like she'd never eaten a day in her life. "I didn't know if you liked cheese on your eggs or not. But then I asked myself, 'Do you know one person who doesn't eat cheese on their eggs?'"

"On everything, I wouldn't have eaten them if the cheese wasn't on them." Tiara smirked up at Stevelle.

He was fully dressed looking just as dapper as he had the day before. He sat down at the end of the bed. The waves on his head were so deep that Tiara couldn't focus on them for too long. She was scared she was going to get lost in them. His chocolate face was so smooth, and the baby-blue shirt he wore accented his broad chest and muscular arms so well that she could see the outline of his six pack. Tiara couldn't help but to imagine how hard and strong he would feel if she was to touch and squeeze him. She quickly tried to shake those thoughts out of her mind. Given what had happened just the night before, she had no business thinking about doing anything with another man. But then again, she had been thinking those thoughts back at the baby shower when she first laid eyes on him. She put her head down and decided to just focus on eating and enjoying the food in front of her. She finished everything on her plate, feeling his eyes burning into her with every bite that she took.

Why is he just watching me like that? I'm broken, she thought.

She's so beautiful, and she doesn't even know it, he thought.

Tiara handed him her empty plate and wiped her hands on her sweatpants.

"Shit."

"What's wrong?" Stevelle asked her, confused by her sudden outburst.

"I didn't pack any clothes from my apartment."

Stevelle stood up from the bed like he hadn't heard anything she'd just said and left the room with the plate.

"OK," Tiara said out loud. "I'll just wear this. Again."

Seconds later, he returned without the plate, but instead, he was holding about ten shopping bags. Tiara peeped them and saw that they were from both clothing and shoe stores.

"Your whole apartment has been cleared out. Everything in it was trashed or donated. I told the manager to do whatever he wanted with it. He agreed to let you out of your lease early under the conditions that he could keep whatever was left inside, and I agreed. So, all the stuff you had in there is gone. I made sure to grab your pictures and shit, though. It's all in a box in the living room. Feel free to go into it whenever you're ready and separate whatever. If there's anything you want to hang up in this room, we'll do it. And as far as clothes and shit, I had Keys go grab you some shit this morning as soon as the stores opened," Stevelle said.

"Keys? You had Keys go shopping for women's clothing?" Tiara said, trying to hide the smile on her mouth, but it read clear as day in her eyes.

"I mean," Stevelle shrugged his shoulders sheepishly, "she one of my boys, but she's still . . . you know, a girl."

Tiara couldn't hold it any longer. She burst out laughing.

"Aw, nah! Let me see this shit. We might have to make another trip!"

"Chill," Stevelle said, placing the bags on the bed so Tiara could rummage through them. "She actually picked out some pretty dope shit. If I woulda went, I woulda had you looking like a wholesome schoolgirl."

Tiara laughed again but was shocked to see that he was telling the truth. Keys had hit her style right on the nail. Everything in the bags was dead-on the head with the hammer.

"Oh my God! She even got the right type of jeans," Tiara said incredulously because it was always hard for her to find jeans that fit both her butt and her waist. "OK, Keys, I see you."

"I'm glad to see you smiling like this," Stevelle chuckled. "I'ma leave you be so you can get dressed. In the meantime, I have some calls to make so I'll be in the living room. Holla at me when you're ready so we can talk real quick."

"A'ight. Wait! Stevelle?"

"What's up?"

"Um . . ." Tiara hesitated with what she was about to ask. "So earlier, you said I could go through the box and take out whatever I wanted to hang up." Tiara gave a long pause.

"Yeah?" Stevelle asked wondering where Tiara was going with this.

"Does this mean you're like . . . letting me stay with you?"

Stevelle looked at her like she was silly and shot her a face. "Duh, nigga, where else you gonna go?" He winked and shut the door behind him.

"Smart-ass," she said under her breath.

"I heard that!"

His voice behind the door made her jump and fall into a fit of giggles. She was definitely feeling him, and she didn't care if she was making it obvious. She wondered what it was about him that had made her like him so much and so quickly. She didn't know if it was the way this little dimple would show on the left side of his cheek when he smiled, or if it was the heartiness in his laugh. Or maybe it was the way he carried himself with a lot of confidence, but somehow was still humble and didn't come off cocky about himself. Whatever it was, it was enough to give her butterflies in her stomach. She wanted to open the door and chase after him like a high school girl, but despite her giddy feelings, she knew they had some serious shit to handle. Her feelings toward Stevelle would have to wait for now because there were bigger fish to fry.

After looking through the bags, she threw on a pair of light blue jeans, some pink and white Nike Roshes, and Nicki Minaj screen T-shirt to match them up.

Stepping out of the room, she joined Stevelle on the couch. He was on the phone when she made her entrance, and he nodded at her to acknowledge her presence. She saw the box he was talking about on the ground. She was glad he had been thoughtful enough to grab her pictures. She didn't have any from when she was younger, but she had made some really good memories with Elaya since they'd escaped the facility. She cherished the few pictures she did have. She sat quietly on his beige love seat patiently waiting for him to finish his call and give her his attention.

"A'ight," he was saying. "Yup, I'm about to find all that out right now, and I'll hit you back a little later." He paused for a second and then laughed. "Yeah, she liked the clothes. She wearing an outfit right now. I'ma holla at you later."

He disconnected the call and put his phone in his pocket.

"So what's up?"

"There's a lot of talk in the streets that that nigga Mario is missing."

Back to reality.

"Damn, that didn't take long. It's only been like one night." Tiara was actually a little bit surprised.

"Well, you gotta remember he was supposed to have killed you, so people were waiting on his call. With him not showing up and shit, they gotta be wondering what the fuck happened to him. It ain't gonna take long for them to figure out he's dead. When that gets out, news of his death most likely will travel fast. What you're gonna have to do for now is lie low. We don't want them to find out you're still alive. It's best for all of us if you just stay ghost and let everybody think you're missing."

"Hell, no." Tiara replied, "I'm not gonna sit here and hide like a little bitch. I'm not afraid of my cousin Vincent or my fucking mother."

"Tiara, this has nothing to do with hiding or letting them think you're afraid of them. This is all about strategizing. With you being missing, it will buy us some time to get our shit ready for the takeover. Once they find out you're still alive, they're gonna lose their motherfucking minds and come after you—except this time, they'll come *twice* as hard; especially since you are the only heir to your father's empire. And you ain't gonna be in hiding forever, just until we ready. Once we have everything set up and ready to go, you show your face, and we take them out. In order for us to get at them, we have to get at them first."

"Your plan would make a lot of sense if you were dealing with a man like how my father was," Tiara stated very matter-of-factly. "My father was a very calm and calculated man. But you're dealing with Vincent. My cousin has always been good with numbers, money, accounts, and paperwork. When it came down to handling shit like this, he was always the one that made quick moves, whether they made sense or not." Stevelle sat back and listened to every word Tiara was saying. It was important for him to get a full understanding.

"The day my father was buried, he told me he planned on moving to New York that same week. This nigga had just been told he had to take over and handle my father's business, and his plan was to leave all this shit and go to another state. I'm telling you this to give you an example of how he functions. Vincent doesn't think his plans through. He thinks on the surface. It's not a good look to let time pass right now. We need to strike while the iron is still hot."

Stevelle looked at Tiara and smiled. She was speaking like a true boss. She was a natural at this. It was obvious that she was her father's child. He had never met Blake Rogers, but he had heard a lot about him, and he knew he had become one of the biggest kingpins in Dallas by taking charge of things and making his own path. It was apparent his daughter was the same way.

"A'ight, Ti, so what's the first move?" He nodded his head at her in agreement with everything she had just said.

"I think it's time I show my face at my child-hood home."

"You sure you ready for that?"

Tiara paused for a second and looked around his home. It was nice, and for him to only be twenty-two, it was clear that he was doing his thing in the streets. Usually, it took a long time for people to earn her trust, but he'd already proven that he would kill for her. As much as it would have been nice for her to stay here with him a little bit longer, she couldn't keep letting time go past her. Gazing into his eyes for a few more seconds, she nodded her head giving him her final OK.

"I don't have a choice. If I don't, they'll just keep coming after me. It's not like I have a fake identity. I am, and will always be, Tiara Rogers no matter where I go, and I'm done running from that. I am the only true Rogers, and my father knew that. That has to be the reason why he left everything to me."

"A'ight," he said. "My niggas will be ready to move tonight. But you still gonna have to lie low for today. Knowing niggas like Vincent, he probably got the whole house on high security, and he probably got everybody in the hood tryna find you or Mario. He probably has a bounty on your head. Follow me."

He grabbed her hand softly, pulled her from the couch, and brought her to the master bedroom of his condo. He let her go when they were in front of his closet and walked in. Inside of it were so many pairs of pants, shirts, and shoes, she understood why he needed a closet so big. That man would never run out of clothes, and that turned her on. There was nothing like a man that could dress his ass off. He complemented her quite nicely.

"If you gon' ride out with me," he said, dragging a large chest from the spacious walk-in closet, "You need a gun."

He popped open the chest and inside it were over fifty firearms. He expected her eyes to pop out of her head when she saw what he was working with, but instead, she eagerly stepped forward. Little did he know, she frequented the gun range. It was the place that she relieved her stress, and she had almost become an expert shot. Since Blake was never able to finish giving her lessons, she took it upon herself to learn. She always used the same gun, and she quickly found the Glock 19 in Stevelle's chest. He was impressed with her choice and gave her an approving nod.

"You sure you know how to—"

He stopped talking as he watched her grab a clip, load the gun, and practice her aim on one of the paintings in the room. When she was done, she let the hand holding the gun hang to her side and used her other hand to point back in the chest.

"Hand me that Mac 19 with that banana clip too, please. I need to borrow a pair of your cargo shorts. All the shit Keys got for me is too tight to conceal shit."

"Okay, so tell us everything that you know about the property."

It was almost eight o'clock, and Stevelle's living room was filled with eight people. She'd already met Mook, Keys, and, of course, Stevelle. She was introduced to Rello, Monty, Teezo, Trent, and Li'l Tay. They all showed her the utmost respect the moment they walked in the house and were all locked, loaded and ready to go.

"There is a gate to get into the community where at least three men stand watch. On the house are rotating security cameras on every side, and each wall has two men manning it. My mother Cat never liked the thought of having my dad's hired hands roaming the house as we slept, so there are none in the house. That's why my father went to the extent of having so much outside security. Nobody can get in that bitch."

"Okayyy." Keys looked at her from where she sat next to Li'l Tay on the couch across from her. "How the fuck we supposed to penetrate that bitch then? If it's sewn up like that."

"Yeah, if shit is that tight, how we gon' get through without being seen?"

Tiara grinned at all of them, and they looked at her like she was a madwoman. She cocked her head and wrinkled her forehead.

"Y'all must have forgotten that I actually lived there for most of my life. My daddy was as strict as they came; he wouldn't let me go anywhere."

"Once again, okayyy," Keys said, not understanding the point that Tiara was getting at. She hoped Stevelle didn't call them over for a rogue mission, because she was the kind of person that valued her time. "What does that have to do with anything?"

"What do kids who are confined to the house do when their parents won't let them do anything?"

Keys pondered the question for a second before the lightbulb went off in her head.

"They sneak out."

"Bingo!"

"We're gonna sneak in through the window in the basement. The only people roaming the house are gonna be the housekeepers."

"What if they aren't there?"

"They will be," Tiara told her.

Before they had all got there, Tiara and Stevelle had sat down and put together an entire game plan. A game plan that she was now explaining in full to the rest of the team. She told all of them the story of how she snuck out of the house to go on a date, and how she got back in the house the exact same way.

"How do you know it will work again?" Li'l Tay asked in a voice a little higher pitched than the rest of the men there. "That was so long ago. They might have fixed the cameras or changed up how they set up their security team."

"I doubt they changed shit up," Tiara responded. "My father set all of that up, and it was practically perfect. I highly doubt Vincent or Cat would change it up even after all of these years. I know it will work," she assured them.

"How though?" Mook asked. "I'm all for backing you up, Princess, but I ain't tryna run into a setup."

"If I know anything about the Rogers, it is that we don't fix anything if it isn't broke, or if we don't know it's broken. I never got caught, which means the blind spot was never found, and I'm positive that even if it isn't the same guard working the post, they have the same habits. At midnight, there is a shift differential; nobody will be manning that post. I'm sure of it."

The room got quiet. She looked around, taking a mental note of the uncertainty that read clear as water on their faces. Suddenly, she felt a surge of rage, and her inner Blake surfaced.

"Y'all are sitting around here like y'all don't trust me," she spoke standing up and talking with her hands. "When really it's me putting everything on the line. Not you. I'm the one with a fuckin' bounty on my head. It's already crossed my mind that any of y'all could have just offed me and collected that money. But I'm standing here putting all my trust in you. So now I need y'all to put your trust in me too. If this shit goes the way I need it to go, I'm going to need each and every one of you around me. I have been through so much *bullshit* in my life, but this? This ain't bullshit to me. This is my legacy, and I need it. I need it just as much as I need y'all; and trust and believe when I take back what's mine and I get on that throne, I will make sure every single one of you is taken care of. I put that on my life."

All of them, including Stevelle, wore shocked expressions, but still nobody said anything. Just when she was about to tell them fuck it and that she was going to go by herself, Keys spoke up.

"Shit, fuck it." She threw her hands up. "I already cancelled my pussy for the night, and I packed enough rounds in the trunk to take out a small army."

"Yeah, man, I'm already here," Monty said. "This could be a good move for me."

"For the record, Princess," Mook's voice filled the living room, "Vincent's money ain't no good. If anybody got close enough to off you, they might as well pick the nearest penny up from off the ground. But then again, if anybody were to get close enough to off you, it would be because they're already dead."

Stevelle, who was closest to Mook, dapped him up and said, "Straight up."

It was set. While the others prepared, Stevelle nodded his head for Tiara to follow him. She glanced back at the others, but they were too busy checking their weapons and sorting out whose mask was whose. She snuck away checking the clock and seeing that it read almost ten o'clock.

"Where are you taking me?" she asked, but he just put his finger to her mouth in response.

He led her out of the front door. When they were in the bright hallway of the building she thought that maybe he wanted to talk to her in private there, he did not stop.

"I wanna show you something," he told her when they were down the hall. He opened a heavy-looking door that was under a big red Exit sign and let her go through first. "Go all the way up."

She did as she was told and trudged up three flights of stairs before she got to a door that said "Rooftop."

"Are we supposed to be up here?"

"Nope," he grinned at her and opened that door too. "But I don't give a fuck."

The chilly breeze hit her face, and she welcomed it, stepping foot on the roof. She panted, trying to catch her breath from walking up all those steps. When they finally reached the top, she lost her breath again when she took in the scenery. The view of Dallas was so beautiful, she felt like she could see everything from where she was standing. She walked until she got close enough to the ledge to look down. From where she stood, she could see dozens of people on the street below her, walking around and enjoying the beginning of Saturday's night life. Cars were driving fast, and the aroma in the air was . . . well . . . Dallas.

"It's beautiful up here.

"Hell, yeah," he agreed with her. He took his place beside her and looked over the city as well.

"Whenever I need to clear my head, I just come up here, spark a blunt, and chill. By the time I go back down to the crib, I usually be cool. There's just something about seeing the city move, you know?"

"So what?" she raised her eyebrow up at him. "You brought me up here 'cause you needed to clear your mind?"

"Kind of," he said with a clenched jaw. "What we're about to do, Tiara, it ain't for play. I just wanna make sure you're ready for what you might have to do."

"I'm ready for whatever."

"Even killing your mother?"

"She practically killed me when she signed her rights over and sent me to that facility. And she tried to have me killed two nights ago," Tiara replied.

"That doesn't answer my question. Will *you* be able to kill *her?*" Stevelle asked the question again.

"I have to do what I have to do," Tiara responded, but she didn't sound as confident as she had sounded downstairs. Stevelle grabbed her by the hands and walked her closer to the edge of the building.

"Look around you. What do you see?"

"I can see everything from here."

"Look down," Stevelle instructed. "What do you see? What do you smell?"

Tiara put her hands in her hoodie and leaned a little bit over the edge of the building. "I see Dallas," she shrugged her shoulder. "I see people, and I smell . . . everything."

"What are those people doing?"

She studied the people moving around care-free like they didn't have any worries in the world. Their laughter carried in the wind, and she was even able to pick up a few snatches of their conversations.

"Living their lives, I guess," Tiara finally answered.

"Exactly," Stevelle turned to Tiara and stared at her deeply in the eyes. "They don't know or care that people like us even exist. They don't give a *fuck*, Tiara. They're living their lives, just like you're trying to do. You're trying to live a life that your mom has tried to take away from you twice. She don't care about you, especially if she can put a dollar on your head. She showed you no mercy. Mario didn't rape you. Your mother did. He was just following orders. So now, what you gonna do about it? When you're put in that position when it's either them or you, what are *you* going to do?"

"I'm-I'm going to have to kill her," Tiara whispered.

"Say it again, Tiara," Stevelle instructed her.

"I'm going to kill that bitch! I put that on my father's grave." She repeated it louder this time.

"Good."

"Yeah, good. I'm still alive, right? After this, I refuse to succumb to that self-loathing feeling again," Tiara said and then got quiet.

Stevelle used that as a window of opportunity to grab her by the waist and brought her to him. "When all of this is over, you won't have to feel that way ever again because I will be here. Right by your side."

"How do you know that? You don't even know me."

"The crazy thing is, I know more about you in two days than I cared to know about girls that I fucked around with for months. I'm not saying I love you or nothing, but I'm saying I think I will one day. There's something about you that seems to have a hold on me."

Tiara couldn't hold his gaze, so she looked at his chest.

"No," she whispered. "I wouldn't want you to love me. You're a good man, Stevelle, regardless of what you gotta do in the streets to survive. You deserve a woman just as good as you. I'm used goods."

"I thought you said you didn't want to self-loathe anymore," he said and placed a finger under her chin. He didn't force her to look at him; instead, he just used his thumb to gently rub her cheek. She'd been forced to do so much, and he wasn't going to be the one to continue that pattern. "I'm not ever going to judge you off your past, shorty. What happened to you was hell, and if I could take all that pain in your heart and put it inside of me, I would. But I can't. All I can do is be here for you and make you smile from here on out. I'll kiss all of your boo-boos away."

Tiara smiled at the way he said, "boo-boos."

"Stop it," she mumbled and tried to pull away from him.

"What?" Stevelle said, kissing her forehead and sending chills down her spine. "I can't kiss your boo-boos?"

His lips were so soft, and Tiara really wanted to lean her head back so that she could feel them on her own. Instead, she pulled away from him and went back to the ledge of the roof. Her eyes were on the traffic below, but she really wasn't looking at anything. A part of her wanted Stevelle so bad. But a part of her felt like he needed to take another pick, and she felt like he needed to know why.

"You know," she started in a barely audible voice, "Mario, the man you killed? I lost my virginity to him back in high school when he was my boyfriend. I gave him the most sacred piece of me to a man with a heart as black as night. He literally took everything from me. Everything."

"Oh, wow."

"Yeah," Tiara said and thought back to that night. "I thought, I just thought—"

"At least you thought," Stevelle interjected. "That's what sets you apart from others."

"Thank you," she whispered, finally looking him back in the eyes.

"Don't thank me for telling you something that you already know."

Something overcame him. It was a like a shock wave in his stomach. He was nowhere near a sensitive man, but the only thing his entire being wanted to do was protect her . . . and kiss her lips. So he did. He leaned down slowly, giving her enough time to pull back if she wanted to. But she didn't. Instead, she placed her arms around his shoulders and cuffed the back of his head with her hands. When their lips met, their bodies meshed closer together. When Tiara closed her eyes, she swore she saw fireworks on the backs of her eyelids.

"Mmm," she moaned in a guilty pleasure when his tongue slid into her mouth.

Her body was giving her confused signals. It was the first time in a long time that she'd been willingly intimate with a man. She was afraid. She thought images of Doctor Pierce and Mario would plague her mind, but surprisingly, they didn't. Any confusion she felt, however, her heart sorted it out for her, letting her know that what she was doing was OK.

She sucked hungrily on his tongue and bit his bottom lip, turning him on and making him wish they didn't have a move to make in less than an hour. If it weren't for his phone vibrating in his pocket, he would have stood there tonguing her down for another five minutes. He pulled away from her, breaking the kiss, and tried to catch his breath before he answered his phone.

"Aye, Chief," Mook's voice sounded on the other end, "we're ready to head out."

"A'ight," Stevelle said and hung the phone up. He looked down into Tiara's doe eyes. "We're going to have to finish this later. It's time to put you back on the throne, Princess."

Chapter 17

The eight of them decided to take two separate cars; two black Toyota Camrys to be exact.

"Some niggas have burned phones," Keys told Tiara as she hopped in the car with her and Stevelle. "My crew has burned cars. We go through these mothafuckas like Swisher Sweets. Plus, nobody is ever gon' suspect a fuckin' Camry dog. These mothafuckas look straight like mom cars."

It took about forty-five minutes for them to get from Stevelle's condo to Blake's community. They drove past the other Camry that was parked a few blocks away from the gate and parked in front of them. When Keys drove past Mrs. Sanchez's place, Tiara remembered going there sometimes after school when she had soccer practice and instantly felt a pang of sadness. Her life growing up hadn't been the worst one. She owned up to the fact too late that she was just a selfish kid. But it was all right because she was about to make up for it. They parked far enough from the gate to not be seen but close enough for their binoculars to reach.

"Get down!" Keys said just in time, and they did as they were told. Their heads ducked down as an Audi A8 pulled past the car they were in. "Shit. I shoulda had Li'l Tay come and case this place earlier."

"It wouldn't have done any good. Cat gets up and leaves at any time of the day. She has never had any kind of schedule. Ever. That bitch's feet are made of wheels."

Tiara leaned up in her seat just in time to see the car go through the gate. Almost ten minutes after that, she had the urge to jump out of the car and just empty her whole clip. She watched as Cat stepped out on the balcony connected to the master bedroom, the one she used to share with Blake. However, she was not alone. Tiara's cousin Vincent trailed closely behind her. She wanted to throw up as she watched Cat being fondled by him with a huge smile on her face. Tiara had to set the binoculars to the side while she tried to stomach what she'd just seen.

"Your moms is foul, yo," Stevelle said, shaking his head. "Not only is she fucking her deceased husband's cousin, but she done moved him up in the crib too. That ain't right."

Tiara silently agreed with him. Her mother had banished her from a home that was rightfully hers and turned her back on her only child. Vincent had promised to always protect her, but his greed was causing him to do just the opposite of that. Deep down, Tiara knew that Vincent might not have really forgiven her father for the mistake he'd made years ago, and at that moment, she regretted saving his life.

"Whoa," Keys said. "She a freak, though. They're fucking hard as shit on the balcony!"

Tiara was disgusted, and Keys saw the look on her face. She shrugged her shoulders sheepishly in a silent apology.

Tiara ignored the statement and put her binoculars back to her eyes to look at the scene taking place. Keys was right, Vincent was tearing Cat up. Tiara's heart wrenched with every delighted expression forming on her mother's face. She had the face of a woman with no problems, still looking young and carefree. At first glance, you would never be able to tell that she was the type of woman to put a hit on her own daughter's head. Or even the type to sleep with her deceased husband's cousin.

"Hopefully, this puts both of them to sleep," Tiara said, looking at the clock in the Toyota they were posted in. It read eleven-thirty. "Almost showtime."

With masks that only showed their mouths securely on their faces, they began to load up and as soon as the clock read eleven forty-five, they made a swift exit. Guns drawn, they ran with Tiara covering the front; Keys in the middle and Stevelle in the back. The others in the car stayed back just as planned and would wait for any signal that backup was needed. They moved with stealth, cloaked by the darkness of the night. By the time they reached the gate, it was five minutes until midnight, and just like Tiara had said, the guard already had left his post.

"Do you remember the code?" Stevelle asked Tiara.

"Of course, I do."

She entered her father's birth month and number in the month, but the final numbers were the year she herself was born. The doors clanked open, and the three of them wasted no time sliding through. Once they were officially on the property, Tiara pulled the gate back closed behind them.

"Come on!" she whispered with urgency, and the three of them ran as fast as they could through the grass. "To the back!"

Tiara pointed at the other two to go toward the basement window. Her body still ached from what had happened to her the night before, but the adrenaline coursing through her blood made it easy for her to ignore the pain. They ducked and dodged the men patrolling the grounds with expertise, but were ready to pop off if anybody was to see them. Finally, when they reached the home stretch, Tiara grabbed both of them roughly by the arms and pulled them behind a bush. While they all ducked, she eyed the rotating camera.

"Damn," Keys panted, "this is the biggest house I've ever seen! And don't get me started on this fucking yard. We moving me in this bitch after all this is over. Got me running like I'm running from the police!"

Tiara didn't respond to anything Keys had just said. She was too busy focusing on the camera and counting the seconds in her head. When she finally got the rotation in her head right, she turned to Stevelle.

"I'm going to go first because I know how to open the window. When I'm through, don't look anywhere else but at me, OK? You will only have ten seconds to get to me. You have to run the exact moment I tell you to. Understand? You too, Keys."

When they both nodded in agreement, Tiara turned her back to them and focused her eyes on the camera. Her timing had to be perfect or else it would only be a futile, and deadly, attempt.

Now! she told herself and took off running as fast as she could.

She counted from zero in her head. It took her four seconds to get to the window, two to push it open, and three more to slide through. She landed hard on her feet, but then lost her balance and fell to her knees. She hurried to get herself back up and pointed her gun around the laundry room. Of course, it was empty. When she was sure the coast was clear, she pushed a crate to the wall under the window. Standing on it, she waved and got Keys and Stevelle's attention.

You have ten seconds, she mouthed to them and did a countdown with three of her fingers while watching the camera.

When the last finger came down, Keys took off running first with the speed of an Olympic track star and slid through the window. Tiara moved out of the way just in time, and Keys landed on her feet.

"OK," Keys said, dusting herself off. "The hard part is over. I bet you fell, huh?" she asked with a huge smirk on her face.

"Fuck you." Tiara stood on the crate and did the exact same countdown for Stevelle.

When he was safely in the house and Tiara was positive that none of them had been detected, she held her gun out in front of her and signaled for them to do the same.

"Follow me," she whispered. "Their room is this way."

Tiara had been right again. The only people roaming the hallways were the housekeepers, and it wasn't too hard to stay out of their way. Tiara was taken back down memory lane when she smelled the aroma of the house. Lavender. It had always been her mother's favorite scent.

They stepped quietly through the house and up the stairs until they reached Cat's room. They held their backs to the wall and tried to listen closely and were able to make out the shower in the bathroom of the master bedroom running. The location of one of the people on the other side of the door was known. Then Tiara heard the familiar sound of her mother's laugh and knew that Cat was probably up watching reruns of *Friends*. Tiara nodded her head to Keys. who stood back aiming at the door while Stevelle prepared to kick it down if needed. They now knew exactly where both of their targets were. Tiara tried the doorknob and burst into the room, gun drawn, and flicked on the light switch.

Cat gasped and tried to scream, but Keys was too quick for her. She slapped her so hard that she fell out of the bed.

"Shut the fuck up, bitch!" she hissed and jammed her gun in Cat's face. "Scream and I blow ya motherfuckin' brains out."

"Is it money you want?" Cat whispered. The color drained from her brown face, and her eyes were open wide like saucers, signifying exactly how scared she was. She was so focused on looking at Keys in front of her that she hadn't even realized that there were other people in the room. "There's a safe in the closet. Take it all!"

"Shut the fuck *up!* Bitch, you're gonna wish, I was just here for money," Keys hissed again, that time hitting her with the butt of her gun.

Blood leaked from her forehead, and she whimpered quietly. Stevelle stood at the door and looked out to make sure nobody came snooping around the corner. He saw how helpless Cat looked, but he knew that bitch had it coming. Cat was cold and heartless. He almost wanted to tell Keys to hit the bitch again. Although she hadn't done anything personal to him, she might as well have. Tiara was one of the most genuine people that he had ever come across in his life, and the fact that these people were trying to break her already broken soul pissed him off.

"Aye," Keys said. "The bathroom."

"Handle that," Tiara told her. "I got this."

Tiara nodded her head toward the bathroom signaling Keys to go grab Vincent from the shower. She then turned her attention back to her mother. Tiara walked up behind Cat, grabbed her by her hair and pulled her to the center of the large bedroom.

"W-who are you," Cat cried. "What do you want?"

"I want you to die," Tiara growled.

"But why? Please don't kill me. My husband, he has more money than you could ever dream of. Whatever you want, it's yours!" Cat was cowering with her head buried into her chest.

Her sobs pissed Tiara off, but not as much as the fact that Cat had just called Vincent her husband.

"You fucking bitch! You married Cousin Vincent?" Her voice was filled with contempt and disgust. Tiara snatched the mask off of her face and shook Cat viciously. "You married your own husband's family?"

Cat gasped. If she was terrified before, the feeling had now tripled. She recognized her daughter instantly, but it was like staring into the face of a ghost. Tiara was the last person that she expected—or wanted—to see. She looked up at her daughter, and all she saw were hateful eyes and a face full of rage. The way Tiara's grip was on her, Cat knew Tiara wasn't there to tell her how much she missed her.

"You are not welcome here!" Cat exclaimed, trying her best to sound brave.

"Bitch, fuck you," Tiara said, hitting her with the butt of her gun. "You got the nerve to tell me I'm not welcome in my own home? This is *my* fucking house—not yours!"

"I don't understand. You were supposed to be dead!"

"And you were supposed to love me and care for me! But I guess shit just didn't work out for either of us. Your plans to have me killed didn't work out, bitch."

"Clearly the little ingrate that killed your father failed at killing you."

"You're nothing but a cold, empty, heartless piece of shit. You're my *mother!*" Tiara kicked Cat in her ribs. "How could you let all of this shit happen? First, you write me off; then you start letting your husband's cousin stick his dick in you? You money-hungry," she said as she kicked her, "bitch! Do you know what I've been through? Do you have *any* idea the kind of hell I went through because of you? All because you didn't take the time to love me and take care of me!"

Tiara proceeded to whoop Cat's ass all around the bedroom. She knocked her into the dresser and made her body bounce off of the closet door a couple of times. The more she hit her, the more Tiara saw that it wasn't enough. Hurting Cat didn't fill the void that was in her heart, so she stopped when she saw that Cat was barely conscious and when she was too tired to land another blow. When she was done, both of her hands throbbed, but she was too doped up on anger to pay attention to the pain.

"And then you move this man in here and let him sleep in the bed you shared with my father? In my father's house? In *my* house? I hate you!" Tiara threw Cat on the ground again. "It's your time to die, Cat. And *I'm* gonna be the one to do it."

Tiara aimed her gun at Cat's head. Cat struggled to lift her head, and for the first time, Tiara saw the guilt in her eyes.

"B-but I'm your mother," Cat said.

"And I'm your daughter," Tiara said. "But that never meant shit to you—did it?"

She pulled the trigger on the silenced gun, and Cat's head exploded right before her face.

"Baby!"

Tiara turned and saw Vincent being brought from the bathroom wearing nothing but a pair of boxers. Keys's gun was on the back of his head, and her hand was on his shoulder. His hands were in the air, but a look of despair crossed his face.

He had seen Tiara shoot his woman, and rage filled him like a helium balloon. He started to charge toward her, but three guns aimed at his head stopped him in his tracks.

"You motherfuckers think you're so slick." The way he spoke to Tiara, she barely recognized him. "I should have known that little motherfucker wouldn't get the job done. I'm glad I hadn't paid him yet."

She'd heard that money changed people, but she never thought that Vincent would be one of those people. He laughed at the way she was looking at him.

"Cat got your tongue, niece?"

"What happened to you, Vincent? You promised to protect me."

"*Money* happened to me, Tiara," Vincent said. "Any other man in my position would have done the same thing."

"But to kill your own family? Your own flesh and blood?"

"If you remember, your dear father tried to kill me years ago. We were family back then too."

"And *I* saved you!" Tiara jerked her gun in his direction.

"Your first mistake," Vincent said icily to her. "Your second mistake was coming in here and forgetting that I, like your father, was raised on the battlefield."

Keys didn't know what hit her when Vincent moved with the speed of a man two times younger than what he was. He grabbed her wrist and made her drop her weapon into his hand. Her arm was straight, and Vincent hit her bone upward at the elbow.

"Aw!" Keys screamed when her bone cracked.

Stevelle tried to get a few rounds off, but Vincent shoved Keys in front of him. One of Stevelle's bullets caught Keys in the shoulder and instantly he drew back. He would forever regret that because Vincent used that as his chance to fire Keys's gun at him.

"Ahh!" Stevelle grunted and clutched himself as he dropped his gun and fell to the ground.

Tiara couldn't tell completely where he'd gotten hit. All she knew was that he was lying still on the ground. She turned back to Vincent and tried to get a clear shot, but she didn't have one, not without hitting Keys again. Vincent head butted Keys with an animalistic grunt, knocking her out cold, and then threw her into Tiara. Tiara dropped her gun, not wanting to let Keys fall to the ground and hurt herself any more than she already was. She tried to set her on her side gently, but before Keys was fully on the floor, Vincent charged at Tiara.

"Thank you for making this easy for me, Tiara," Vincent said, grabbing her by the neck and kicking her gun away from her hand's reach. "I needed you dead, and you came straight to me! With as strong of a vengeance that you have right now, I can only assume your stupid-ass little boyfriend told you everything."

Vincent spun her around and put her into a choke hold. Tiara tried to say something to him, but she couldn't. Her hands flew to his muscular arms and his face in a futile attempt to poke out his eyes. Her eyes fell on Keys and Stevelle, regretting that she had even let them come on the mission with her. She reached out for her friends. She was afraid that they were dying. She was overcome with guilt.

"I'm going to kill them," Vincent whispered so closely in her ears that Tiara felt the moistness from his breath. "But you won't get to see that. I'm gonna kill *you* first." He squeezed a little harder, and she gasped, trying to get air, but her airway was completely blocked.

"It wasn't supposed to turn out like this, you know. I never planned for any of this to happen. You are my niece, and I loved you like a daughter, but you see, I have my own daughter. She has your old room actually. I have responsibilities, and honestly, this is the way that Blake Rogers can truly pay me back for what he did to me all those years ago."

Everything around Tiara seemed to fade away, and she knew she was losing her grip on life. Her eyes shut, and she was about to succumb to her death when she heard Vincent grunt in pain behind her and felt his grip on her loosen.

"Get off of her!"

Tiara collapsed on her side and gasped for breath. Her throat felt like it was on fire with every breath she took, but her lungs were happy to be filled with oxygen again. She rolled on her back and felt gentle hands touch her face tenderly.

"Oh, Tiara, I knew I heard your voice," Stephanie said, turning her back on Vincent and kneeling beside Tiara. "I thought you'd never come home."

In her hand, she was holding a bloody broken vase. Behind her, Tiara saw Vincent struggling back to his feet. Tiara tried to warn Stephanie, but it was too late. Vincent sent one of his fists crashing into the side of Stephanie's face. He hit her a few more times before standing up straight. Tiara looked around and saw that she was within arm's reach of the gun that Keys had dropped.

"I never liked that bitch!" Vincent grunted and went to finish Stephanie off.

"And I'm sure the feeling is mutual," Tiara said, holding the gun up.

When Vincent realized he'd made a big mistake turning his back on Tiara, he tried to lunge for her, but she was too quick for him. She let one shot off and caught him in his right shoulder. She tried to fire another round, but he jumped out of the way just in time. Right then, she heard an array of gunshots going off in the lower level and knew that could only mean one thing: the guards had realized there was a breach in security, and they had sent backup.

"Boss!" she heard a gruff voice yell from the entrance of the bedroom, and she jumped to the side just as automatic rounds went off and tore the room up.

She hid on the side of the bed and fired aimlessly, hoping she'd at least hit one person. Realistically, though, she knew she most likely wasn't hitting anybody. That stuff they showed in the movies wasn't real. The chances of you aimlessly firing a gun in a room and actually hitting anyone was slim to none.

"Boss, let's go," the voice said again. "There are too many of them! The chopper is landing in two minutes. We need to get you out of here!"

Tiara stuck her head up from the side of the bed, and the man with the automatic weapon saw the top of her head. He sent an array of shots her way. One of them caught her in her right arm, and she gasped loudly, falling to the floor. The pain was one that she'd never felt before. It was like a searing burn that was constant. She held her arm with her left hand and scooted away from the spot where she was just at. Feathers from the pillows that the shooter had just shot up floated everywhere in the air, making it hard for him to see exactly where she had gone. But when she peeked around the corner of the bed, she looked just in time to see Vincent pointing at Stevelle, who was moving slightly on the ground.

"Grab him! He goes with us!"

"Noooo!" Tiara screamed and tried to get to her feet to stop them. But she dropped back down when the rapid gunfire rang out again. When she was finally able to get up, they were gone.

Not knowing what else to do, she scooted on the ground to where Keys lay and tried to hold her in her arms. Her arm still felt like it was on fire, but she didn't care. Holding Keys in her arms reminded her of when she'd held Brandy. It felt like that had been so long ago.

She removed the mask from Keys's face and cringed at the sight of her nose. It was bloody and looked like it was broken.

"Keys, please don't die on me," Tiara said and then looked back over her shoulder at Stephanie, who was groaning and holding her head.

"That son of a bitch hit me!"

Tiara breathed a sigh of relief. She was happy that Stephanie was alive. She looked back down at Keys and nudged her. That time she got some movement. Keys moaned and opened her eyes slowly. The first thing she saw was Tiara's somber face.

"Whoa," she said. "You don't look so good."

"Neither do you, bitch." Tiara looked at Keys's broken arm and knew she would need medical attention ASAP. "Can you move?"

Keys nodded her head and winced as she tried to get to her feet. She was light-headed, and the pain in her arm was so powerful that it felt like her whole body had become numb. But she'd take a broken arm over a gunshot wound any day. Keys realized she was covered in blood, but she knew it couldn't have all been hers. She looked at Tiara, and that's when she realized Tiara was bleeding profusely from her arm.

"Damn, T," she said, alarmed. "That nigga got you. I hope you got him back worse. We need to get to the hospital or something. Where's Stevelle?"

She could tell by the way Tiara was looking at her that something very bad had happened. Her first thought was to pray that he hadn't gotten killed. But then she hazily remembered Vincent shooting him. She frantically scanned the floor for his body.

"What happened to Stevelle, T?" she asked when she didn't see him anywhere. "Where the fuck is he?"

"They took him," Tiara said, fighting back her tears.

"He-he's not dead," Tiara told her. "They took him. Vincent took him."

Keys didn't have the chance to say anything because suddenly the bedroom was swarmed with men with automatic weapons. Tiara recognized some of them from when she was a teenager; others were new faces. Their guns were pointed at everyone in the room, but once one of them recognized Tiara, their guns were dropped instantly.

"Princess," one of the men called out. It was what all of Blake's soldiers called her. She felt relieved and knew she was safe. "You probably don't remember me, but I have known you since you were a little girl. My name is—"

"Frank," Tiara finished. "I remember you. Vaguely, but I remember your name."

"Are you OK? What happened?" Frank asked looking at Cat on the ground with half of her face blown off.

"I was shot. Vincent shot me," Tiara said. "And my friend, she needs medical attention. Cousin Vincent and my mother tried to kill us. So I had to do what I had to do."

Frank was silent for a second while he studied Tiara's face, perhaps looking to see if she showed any signs that she was lying. When he saw the tears streaming down her face and the sadness and exhaustion in her eyes, he knew she was telling the truth.

"I knew something wasn't right about her when she didn't bring you back home after your incident," he sighed.

The man looked back at the others and used one finger to point at Cat's dead body. "Get this bitch's body out of here. The rightful heir to the empire is home. Make sure Vincent never steps foot on this property again. Get an ambulance here pronto for these girls and line up those young thugs downstairs."

"Young thugs?" Tiara instantly knew who Frank was talking about. "Are they OK? I mean, are they alive?"

"Are the alive? Those motherfuckers killed half of our people in security! Are they with you?"

"Yes," Tiara nodded her head. "Please don't hurt them. They only busted in here like that because they thought something bad had happened to me. Those are my people."

"This is your show now, Princess," Frank told her. "You tell me those are your people, I'll respect that. I wouldn't do a thing to harm them. Plus, with you back, I can finally retire because you can sign my check! I'm too old for this shit. I'm a good shot, but the only shot I want to take is one that contains whiskey. Those boys did their damn thing tonight. Those soldiers downstairs can take my spot." He stopped and looked at Keys. "Not her, though. She needs to get her weight up."

Keys glared at Frank who burst into laughter.

"Welcome to the life of being a kingpin's bodyguard," he said and then looked at Tiara. "It's good to have you home, Princess."

With that being said, he left the room. Although Stephanie was dinged up pretty badly, to the point where she too needed medical attention, she fretted over Tiara and Keys like they were her own children. She grabbed towels and tried to clean the girls until the ambulance arrived. Tiara and Keys filled the boys in on what happened, and they left as soon as they could to see what they could find out on the streets. They knew the streets would be talking a mile a minute.

When the EMTs finally arrived, they allowed Stephanie to walk to the ambulance but forced Keys and Tiara to get on stretchers. Tiara requested that Stephanie ride with her, She'd missed her so much, and she didn't want them to be separated. One of the paramedics was about to speak when he was interrupted by the sound of a woman yelling. Tiara immediately recognized the voice and looked to where it was coming from. From where she lay on the stretcher on the circular driveway in front of the house, Tiara looked to the gate where she saw a very pregnant Elaya and Clarence waving at them, trying to get their attention.

"Tiaraaaa!" Elaya yelled. "Let me through this *fucking gate right now!*"

Tiara knew it was in her best interest to allow Elaya through. She looked toward her security and told them that it was OK to let them through. The man at the gate opened it for Elaya, and she gave him the dirtiest look that she could muster.

"I told you I know her!" Elaya huffed and moved fast for a pregnant woman. She finally reached the ambulance where her friend was in and fought the urge to slap her. "See! This is why the fuck I'm glad I activated the tracker on your cell phone, bitch! You were supposed to call me yesterday! I have been blowing you up and worried out of my damn mind! I went over to your apartment, and it was cleared out, and now look at you! All bruised up. I thought-I thought—"

Suddenly she burst into tears and fell on Tiara lying on the stretcher. Tiara winced at the pain but didn't think it would be wise to ask Elaya to get off of her.

"'I'm all right, Elaya. I promise."

"I thought you were dead!" Elaya pulled away from her and placed a swollen hand on Tiara's cheek. "I could beat your ass right now. Whose house is this? And why are you here?" She glanced over and saw Keys watching the whole exchange. "And who the fuck is she? Let me find out you're caught in a lesbian love triangle and her bitch caught y'all! *Whose house is this?*"

"It's mine," Tiara said weakly. "This is the Rogers's estate."

Elaya's eyes grew wide open, and she swiveled around to get another look at the house.

"Damnnnn," she said and then turned back to Clarence. "Baby, I'm going to ride in the ambulance with Tiara. You go and ride with her girlfriend, OK?"

The EMTs hoisted Tiara up in the back, and Elaya clambered in too. Stephanie sat next to Elaya as well. It was a little tight, but somehow, they made it work.

"OK," Elaya eyed her friend suspiciously, "what the hell is going on?"

"Let's just say," Tiara grabbed Elaya's hand in hers and made a kissing gesture at Stephanie before they shut the door to the ambulance she was in, "everyone who has ever wronged me got what they deserved."

Elaya looked from Tiara to Stephanie.

"I'm sorry to curse in front of you, ma'am," Elaya said to Stephanie before turning to look at her friend, "but, bitch, let me just say, you got me all fucked up right now!" Elaya exclaimed, and then got the attention of the paramedic. "Umm, you plan on telling your driver to start driving? My friend is looking all types of ways messed up, and this woman looks pretty banged up too. I believe they are ready to go."

The paramedic shut the door on them, and the three ladies rode in silence for a few seconds.

"Now, what *really* happened?"

"Fuck that," Tiara said, staring at Elaya like she had laser vision. "When the fuck did you put a tracker on my phone?"

"Girl," Elaya waved her hands like what her best friend had just said was totally irrelevant, "I did that months ago. I don't know what I would do without you. When I went to your apartment yesterday and saw that it was empty, I almost called the police, but instead, I tracked you. Now, look at you. You're too pretty to be looking fucked up like that, child. Oh my God, if I would have lost you I would have died."

"Stop it," Tiara said soothingly. "You're going to upset my babies and go into early labor, and I really don't want to hear Clarence's mouth."

"I'm cool, I'm cool," Elaya said. "Now, tell me what happened!"

Tiara knew Elaya wouldn't let anyone live unless she knew the events of that night. So she told her. The one part she left out was the rape that had taken place at her apartment. She didn't want to get Elaya upset about that. That was the last image she wanted in Elaya's mind, and she wasn't sure if she'd be able to handle it. When she was done telling the story, it felt like all of the energy she'd regained was gone again.

"Wow, T," Elaya said. "Your own mom?"

"Yeah," Tiara said. "Crazy thing is, I don't feel nothing. When I pulled the trigger, it felt like I was killing a complete stranger. If anything, Stephanie here has been more of a mother to me than Cat ever was." Tiara looked over at Stephanie who looked down lovingly at her.

Elaya nodded her understanding.

"So . . . Does that mean this is over? Once and for all?" Elaya asked them as she looked at Tiara.

Tiara lowered her gaze to the ground. She wished she could say it was over, but that would be far from the truth. She now held a solemn expression on her face.

"What? Why are you looking like that? You don't have any more crazy assassins coming after you, do you? Or do you think Vincent will come back to steal your inheritance? You said he escaped, right?"

"Yeah, he got away. And the answer to your other questions is, probably both," Tiara swallowed and gave Elaya a look that let her know that she was done answering questions for the night.

Epilogue

One month later

The day was sunny when she made her way through the cemetery. It was the first time that she'd ever been able to muster up enough courage to show her face at his grave site since he'd been buried. It blew her mind that even from the grave years later, Blake still intimidated her. His tombstone was a large angel, bigger than any of the others in the cemetery, and he was separated from the other burials at the grave site. It was a nice winter day, and the air was rigid, but that didn't stop Tiara from making footprints in the snow to get to her father.

She was breathing slightly heavy when she finally reached the spot where her father was buried and put her hand on the cold tombstone to wipe some of the snow away. She read the words that were engraved.

Here lays Blake Alexander Rogers. A loved husband, father, and businessman. May he rest peacefully in the arms of forgiveness.

"Hey, Dad," Tiara said and kissed the tombstone. She felt a breeze on her cheek, and she smiled. "I know, I know. What took me so long, right? I'm sorry."

Tiara knelt down and talked like her father was kneeling right in front of her, in the flesh.

"I just wasn't ready to come see you," she said. "It took me awhile to come to terms with all of this. I never meant for you to die, Dad."

Tiara took a deep breath. She thought everything in her life would fall into place once she embraced who she truly was, but it turned out that it was both a blessing and a curse. There was still no word on Stevelle, and the biggest piece of her heart prayed that nothing too terrible had happened to him. She prayed to God every day that he was still alive. After all, it was thanks to him that she'd even gotten her father's empire back.

She'd jumped headfirst into all of her father's business dealings, even the illegal ones. In only one month, she had revamped his entire operation. With an array of killers by her side that would go if she gave the order, she had no worries about anybody testing her. She learned as she went, and each day she grew *a little more gangster. No longer was she that naive green girl that she once had been. Soon, her name would ring bells the same way her father's had. She was doing good by Blake Rogers's name and proved that she not only looked like him, but she had his hustle too. She moved back into the house that she'd grown up in, and it took a little getting used to, but after completely redecorating the entire house, minus the basement, she started to feel at home again.*

Elaya visited often, even though Tiara told her to stay her phat ass at home. She was due any day now, and the only thing she should have been doing was resting up before she wasn't allowed to sleep for the next eighteen years.

Through all of her successes, she felt like something wasn't right in her life. She had forgiven Doctor Pierce for all of the horrible things he had done to her. She had even forgiven Mario for what he'd done to her. But still, something wasn't settled in her life. Tiara still visited her counselor once a week, and from seeing Tiara for years, he seemed to know exactly what was missing in her life. He told her that she would never be at peace with her past until she faced her last demon. At first, she started to call this ridiculous, but when she thought about it, she knew he was right. So there she stood.

"I saw your video," Tiara said. "The video of your death. Frank showed it to me before I signed his final check. I heard your last words, and it meant everything to me to know that you didn't hate me. But still, that didn't make me hate myself any less for what happened. Your death was my fault. I let Mario into your home, into the home you built from the ground up to protect you from the kind of harm I inflicted! Oh, Daddy, I would do anything to have you here with me. There is still so much that I don't know. I never knew until now how much I needed you. I wish we could have another chance, but unfortunately, that's not the way things can be. But I love you with all of my heart."

Tiara felt another breeze. That one seemed to linger on her cheek, almost as if it were caressing it. A tear came to her eye, but she quickly wiped it away, remembering that her father hated to see her cry.

"Anyway, I have tons of news for you," she said. "I finally am happy. I'll spare you the gory details of what has happened to me up until now. We all know how your anger is. I made a new friend, though. She's amazing. Elaya is the nicest person that you'll ever meet. She can *sometimes have an attitude problem, but that's usually in the morning. She is pregnant with twins right now, so her nerves are really bad, but that's what tequila is for, right? Let me stop. Her pregnant behind won't be able to drink for a while right now."*

Tiara giggled a little bit.

"Her husband is my lawyer. You should see how much work I've been moving. Vincent fucked up the operation something crucial. He didn't know much more than I do, but even I know you don't sell the type of product we have for half just to make a quick sale. The difference between him and you, Dad, is that you worked to feed a village. He, on the other hand? Worked to feed himself. I am about to close one of the biggest heroin and Ecstasy deals this state has ever seen.

"I met another girl. Her name is Keys, and she's mad cool. She actually plays for the same team. Before you say anything, we are just friends! She's a fighter. You would like her. Her loyalty speaks volumes, and I know that if I were to go against the world at this very minute, she would be right by my side. I won't tell you exactly what bonded us; just know that we are literally bonded by blood. I love them both like my sisters, and I'm blessed to have them in my

life. Stephanie is still around the house fussing at me. She disagrees with me taking over parts of your business, but I'm a Rogers. It's only right. I'll be having to take a few months off, though, to help Elaya with the babies."

Tiara smiled sadly and pictured the surprised look that she knew would have spread across her father's face.

"Yes, Daddy," she said. "I met somebody. He's a good man, and now, just like what happened with you, something has happened to him because of me. I think about him so much, and I think I love him; very much, actually. I don't know if he loves me, but I do know that he doesn't care about any of what happened in the past. He's the one that helped me take back the throne. He gave me a fresh start. You would like him. He's smart, and he is a street pharmacist like you. Not scared to brandish a gun and gets it popping in the streets. I just pray that he's OK."

Tiara reached into the pocket of her Alexander McQueen coat and grabbed a wad of cash that totaled $1,000.

"OK, Dad," she said. "That's enough for now. I would have brought you flowers, but I thought you'd like this more. I'll come back next week. I love you. Oh, and I'm sorry for killing your wife. She wasn't shit, though."

She kissed his tombstone and stood to her feet. There was one other person that she had come to visit. She left her father's grave and took a few minutes to find the one she was looking for. When she found it, she felt her heart skip a beat. The gravestone there was an angel as well, but it was small. She did just like she'd done with her father's tombstone and wiped the snow away.

Here lies Brandy, beloved daughter, sister, and friend. When all hope seems lost, hope some more. Forgive and always put love out into the world, because you only get what you give out.

Tiara choked on a sob because she could hear her best friend saying those exact words. She didn't care about the snow. She dropped to her knees and hugged the tombstone.

"Hi, sister," she whispered and let her tears fall freely. "I miss you. I would tell you everything that's happened to me until now, but I have a feeling you already know. I was raped, beaten, and almost murdered, but I made it through it all. I guess that means that I'm meant to be where I am today, huh? You were always stuck on your philosophical shit. I feel horrible standing here alive while you're here buried. But knowing you, I know you're at peace. You were always the stronger one."

Tiara shut her eyes and remembered Brandy's radiant smile, the hugs and kind words that she gave Tiara during tough times. Tiara thought of Brandy every day, and every time she thought of her, she still couldn't believe that she was gone.

"I kept your promise." Tiara pulled away from the tombstone. "It may have taken me awhile to get the guts to come up here, but I never forgot about you. Not even once. I mean, who could? You were the best friend a person could hope to have. Elaya would have loved you. You would fit in perfectly just because we all love to laugh. I have some more news for you, though."

Tiara smiled and heard Brandy's voice in her head saying, "Okayyyyy . . . I'm waiting!"

"There is a lot that I have to do to make peace with myself and with the world. The man that I think I love was snatched away from me . . . I don't even know if he's alive. I have already spent a quarter of a million dollars looking high and low for him; just can't find it in me to believe that he's dead. Why would Vincent take him to just kill him? It doesn't sit right with me."

Feeling a queasiness in her belly, Tiara cradled her stomach and stopped talking for a second. That often happened when she thought too hard about Stevelle. The fact that somebody could be harming him because he'd chosen to stand firm by her side ate her up. Keys and Monty did their best to keep her on the bright side. They often told her that if he was alive, he would turn up, and if no dead body turned up, then they would assume he was alive and keep looking. She blinked back the tears and decided to change the subject.

"So my friend Elaya . . . She's having twins. She's going to name one of them Brandy. It just has a ring to it, don't you think?" Tiara said and let her fingers gently brush against the tombstone. "I love you, Brandy, always and forever."

Tiara said her good-bye, promising to visit her whenever she came to visit her father. She stood up and turned her back on both of them to make her way back down to where her car was waiting. She walked slowly in the snow toward the silver Mercedes-Benz that she'd purchased for Keys. She was so lost in her thoughts that she didn't even notice that Keys was standing outside of the car with an alarmed look on her face.

"What's wrong?" Tiara asked her, wrapping the ties on her peacoat tighter on her small waist. "You burnt a hole in the leather of your car already?"

When Keys didn't even crack a smile, Tiara knew something was extremely wrong. Hanging loosely from her hand was Tiara's cell phone. The screen was still lit up, and Tiara made a curious face at her.

"What the fuck is wrong with you? Why you acting so weird? And why do you have my phone? I don't go through yours, so don't go through mine."

Keys and Tiara had gotten close like sisters. After finding out that Keys was living in a one-bedroom house in the hood, it was nothing to move her onto the Rogers's estate. Keys and Stevelle had been closer than anyone else in their crew. It made Tiara feel safer and like she had a piece of Stevelle with her.

"Here." Keys was zombielike as she handed Tiara her cell phone. "I-It's my bro."

"Stevelle?" Tiara exclaimed with excitement in her voice and snatched the phone from Keys. "Where is he? Does he need us to pick him—"

When she saw what was on the screen, she stopped mid-sentence.

"No," she whispered. "No!"

She caught a sharp breath of brisk air and looked from the phone to Keys with wavering eyes. On the screen of the phone was a picture.

It was of a man hanging from his arms in what looked like a meat cellar. The man was almost naked. All he wore was boxers, and his body was beaten up so badly and covered with cuts. It was Stevelle. Along with the picture message, there was a regular text message.

If you want your friend to stay alive, you will do exactly as I say, my dear cousin. Not only will you pay me $1 million in both cash and product, you will take over my contract with Rodriguez and pay him back all that I owe. You have twenty-four hours to get me my first request. If I don't have it after sending this message, I am going to slit your boyfriend's throat. If Rodriguez is not paid in one week's time, he is going to come after all your peoples, and after he's done killing all the ones that you love, he's gonna come after you.

When Tiara was done reading the text message she walked calmly to the passenger-side door. She opened it and got in without a word. Keys followed suit and put the car in drive so that they could pull off from the burial site.

"So, what's our move? Are you really going to pay that nigga all of that money? Just give him work?"

"I can't let him die."

"That's a setup," Keys said. "He's trying to punk you out and make you look weak to the other empires."

"I know."

"That nigga ain't gon' do shit but snake you in the end."

"I know!"

"Then what?"

Tiara sighed and clenched her eyes shut. She had only been at the head of the table for a month, and already she had to make a life-or-death decision. With a clenched jaw, she made a choice right then and there not the bow down to a man, not even on her level of anything.

"I'm not going to let him die," she said.

"So you're going to pay up?" Keys scoffed.

"Hell, no," Tiara told her, and then looked out the window as Keys drove.

The snow was a funny thing. It would come down and stay for a little while, but once it got under some heat, it would melt away.

Much like her enemies would learn to do.

"What are you saying then?"

"I'm saying that we have twenty-four hours to find Stevelle and kill Vincent. And we have one week to prepare to go to war with Rodriguez."